The Commitment Act

and Other Stories

Shawn Miller

DEDICATION

For the talented Em, and for my parents

CONTENTS

WHAT YOU'RE UP AGAINST NOW

The first note might show up in your mailbox at work. You know, the one you check off and on or get your secretary to check on her way to get coffee in the morning, if you're lucky that way. It won't be anything special, just a simple piece of laminated mail you'll use to write a note on from your boss later that day because he doesn't always wander into your office, but when he does you've got to take a note as quickly as you can, and the laminated mail is the only piece of scrap within your reach. Then when's he gone and you can finally let a breath out for passing the most recent test of the day you'll flip over the laminated piece of junk and actually read what's on the card.

You're single, or maybe just in a relationship where you feel you will be in only a matter of moments. Or you're with one of those partners that likes the thrill of bending a connection until it snaps into little pieces at the pairs of your separate feet, the smile on their face a sign of terrible things to come ahead. What does it mean to truly find what we're all really looking for in this life? We run and run and run around complaining about the rent, about the news, about the neighbor next door who won't turn down his television set when the clock strikes midnight. We run, but who do we run to? Life isn't sustainable on just one set of feet, one pair of legs. Life needs balance, and the only way to not fall flat on your face is to find that other pair of legs to lean into. That's what the laminated card represents, or at least that's what's printed on it when you flip over the note your boss had you take.

When the first advertisements for LifeTime, or it's commonly referred to moniker LT, hit the market, everyone believed it was a scam. We'd already had our share of dating companies fighting for the money in our pocket, and when LifeTime's creator Harrison Ryerson promised the opportunity to truly find the one and only this ridiculously large world offered you by simply answering a list of questions and then staring into a webcam or, if you didn't have one available, your phone's camera through the LT App, one could reasonably be as distrusting as you'd expect. The few fools there were would go in and try it, see it for what it was and tell the rest of the world in online forums, blogs, and review videos that would ultimately shut down LT for once and all. Except that never happened, and now, seven years after LT's creation, all I keep getting are these laminated ads thrown into my mailbox reminding me how alone I've become.

Not having a pet, now that'll probably help get you on LT's doorstep, but then again they have new Pet Days for their members. Or deciding after work to not hit up one of the hook-up bars along Stephens and 7th they helped to fund back three years ago when they felt they were not creating enough happiness in the world by just having an online presence in communities. Hell, any kind of non-communication usually gets you put on some sort of spam list they throw out. Perhaps you'll get home one evening, take-out bag thrown over your wrist like a misplaced tattoo and, reaching into your home's mailbox this time, feel the glossy cover of a LifeTime magazine gracing the inside of your palm. Never realized how smooth everlasting love could feel until it gets delivered to your doorstep.

Used to be you'd go to a bar and try your luck, come back home and laugh to yourself through a buzzed memory of rejection coupled with a bill that might have been just a tad too high for your liking. Throw your keys on the side table you thought looked good at the department store down the street the week before when, just like tonight, you wandered into your home alone too scared of what the future might look like to bother opening your eyes this one time and instead spend all that worthwhile attention on a place to rest your keys and sometimes your wallet. That's where LT steps in, to fix your attention on what really matters: love.

You've got to understand, life has become much simpler than it used to be. We aren't robots necessarily, but when LifeTime became a reality, a legitimate piece of romantic material that wasn't just a dating website dangled in front of the lonely, well, things changed. People handed over their money and suddenly they were handed back a legitimate face, another person that supposedly was their SoulMate, listing their name, their location, their email address on the back of the picture. Breaches of privacy had long flown out the window, so why wouldn't it seem possible a company run by the government for, as they called it, the "betterment of its people" have access to very private information? Loads and loads of information, all thrown together to form what makes LifeTime so appealing. LT could find you happiness.

At first it seemed fake, real easy to fake looking at it now. Phone number could just go to one of the sex hotlines possibly, or maybe to an actor hired by LT working in their corporate offices. Be kind of fun that way, to talk with a fake. But the one-time fee, that threw people off. Usually monthly fees, subscriptions, payments, all the sort. They wanted to bleed you, not just take a prick and walk away. LifeTime did it differently though, and then the stories started.

Forums, online communities and the like were the first places you heard from. "Only $39.99, so I thought I'd give it a go. My heart ain't getting any younger, right? But this was different." Or it was, "The price was cheap so I was worried my payment info would be comprised. Taken for a ride. Not LT. Found my Richard through them the first week. Gave my money and suddenly the face of a man I'd never met popped up in my mailbox that Wednesday. My SoulMate it said, as if I should've known before."

The news outlets would pick up the story next, eager beavers locking into a story that could make people smile, people forget about the murders on at 6, 6:10, and instead turn their focus to this fun new company out of our nation's capital. "Have you ever believed you might have missed out on love? What if the man bagging your groceries could be the man you marry? Or the woman walking alongside you on the sidewalk, could they be Ms. Right? A new start-up named LifeTime has found a home online as a place where people don't just fall in love but are given the exact information on how to find the love of their live. May sound crazy, but let's go to our own Dr. Love, Dan Fitzgerald, to see how we all can get bitten by the love bug."

People protested at first, as should be the case. Breach of security, government involvement, the whole nine yards. The voices were strong, the public angry at what they felt was more a dictatorship than a democracy, and for a time it felt like maybe it would've worked. But then, happiness all over. Too many of those voices started paying the $39.99 fee, to see if they could poke the giant, government controlled love machine past the edge. Find the wrongs and not the rights, become a populace not fit for the brainwashing they felt had begun spreading its tiny fingers all over the country.

And then of course, they got the package in the mail that Wednesday. They'd feel the outside of the perforated yellow envelope, attempting to convince themselves that it wasn't real. All a joke, all a silly little joke. Scissors in one hand, the package in the other. Careful when they cut, in case they could use the information later to spoil the government's plans. Fighters they were, right up until the picture would fall out onto the floor. They'd see the face, and that's when the fight left their body.

There's a whole bunch of silly little sayings on what love looks like when you see it. Time could stop, or that first sight is enough for the rest of your life, because you know what you're up against now. Wedding bells, whatever those might be, start rattling in your mind like a jingle you heard on the radio on your way home from work. These freedom fighters, the ones convinced the government was wrong for taking their identities and using them on a website fit for love, immediately felt a wave wash over them when they first laid sight on that photograph. No longer wrong was the "Man" for using what they not ought to. No longer would they yell in front of the White House, in front of Capitol Hill. No longer would they shake their heads as they listened to the creator of LT, Harrison Ryerson, discuss on CNN how the only reason LifeTime was given a chance to exist was because "love deserved more than people could provide." Nothing else mattered now that their SoulMate was staring at them from the ground beneath their feet. A handpicked individual just for them, as if God reached out and anointed them a lover Himself.

The theory holding the company up for so long before the nation gave in was fascinating from an outsider's perspective. A private, government-funded project dipping its ugly head into the general population should be easily drowned, but the power it held over those in the country helped keep it afloat. Love conquers all, now there's a silly little line that proved to be far too truthful. Love did conquer all, LifeTime shedding its "bad guy" image as the stories turned into reality. The average citizen, 18 years and older, could with forty bucks not have to go through the pain and torment of a break-up or divorce. They could find the one they were meant to be with, until death, and escape the anguish. LT was by all accounts a miracle. But of course, nothing could be that easy, right?

Pain, in fact, did follow as LT grew. Pictures in the mail meant that your spouse, your partner, might not be the one you were meant for. Divorce courts jammed to the gills, people spilling out of the doors. Families torn apart, lives destroyed at the prospect of another. Violence, all the violence. Blood spilt was for a good cause this time people thought, because remember: love conquers all. They were SoulMates, and SoulMates sometimes had to fight through what already existed to be together. LifeTime had a pickle on its hands, but only for a moment. This wasn't your typical dating website, after all.

The population has found happiness, for the most part. Statistics spewed out on news websites and on television networks have nearly 60% of the United States currently in love through LifeTime. Hell, you could just go to LT's home page and see for yourself. "You deserve more" in neat letters underneath a large, bold set of letters, the L slightly bigger than the T, but not by much. 60 percent, now that's just a number. There's still the other 40, right?

Gives me hope that maybe people aren't just giving up on the bar, the subway, the park for Christ sakes. Leaves me a chance to do it the right way I suppose. Not break up a family when my SoulMate turns out to be a thirty-five year old mother of three. Don't have to send the kids to one of the LifeTime Child Care facilities ("You deserve a chance to start over") because I need time with the one I discovered I love from a picture that fell at tips of my shoes one rainy, Wednesday evening.

I may be bitter because I like to imagine I find my wife over a drink at the bar rather than through a click of my mouse. Our eyes will meet, I'll wander over to her side and ask if she'd like another. She'll smile, pat the back of my hand softly, gently, and say sure, if I'm offering. I'll smile, maybe let out a quick chuckle, and raise my hand towards the barkeep, two fingers held high. We could be perfect, or we could be terrible. But what's the fun in love if all I have to do is check my mailbox at work, at home, and give my credit card information?

$39.99 might buy you happiness, but what if you paid the money, checked on that Wednesday, carried the package eagerly up the stairs and fumbled your keys and couldn't help but let out a small yelp of joy, thinking the lonely nights were over. Thinking you'd take your scissors, cut carefully along the edge and let the picture fall to the floor, facedown to let the moment build and build and build until you reached down and picked it up, the LT watermark on the back letting you know, letting you see that it was real. That your money wasn't just wasted, that this might be it. Was she a redhead? A blonde? Or would it be a nice, slender brown haired woman, a gentle face that screamed love forever at you?

The happiness that had eluded you each morning as your secretary brought you a coffee, black with no cream. The happiness that had left you when your father passed, when your mother died. When your brother, your only fucking brother, leaving your sight one last time because you weren't worth the time anymore, now that our parents had left for good. You've waited forever for this forever, and now this company with their silly little love lines, their laminated pieces of junk mail, their stupid bullshit magazines, they'd brought it to you directly, all for less than a fifty dollar bill. Your hands are shaking, your tongue heavy, your brow sprouting sweat. You've lived this life of frozen meal weekdays and drunken weekends long enough on your own. Now is the time to start over. And then you flip the picture over.

I think I'm bitter because I don't want to break-up a family. I think it's because I want to lock eyes with my girl, yes my girl, over a beer at a seedy bar uptown. I make up these excuses in my head because when I saw the LifeTime logo on the front of the yellow envelope, my heart rose as if I was already engaged to be married. When I took my flimsy pair of scissors and began cutting the top of the envelope I worried for a moment that I might chop off my beloved's right eye or ear by mistake. The picture fell on top of my crusty black dress shoes and the LT logo on the back radiated in the dim light given off by the kitchen in my apartment. I laughed, thinking this would be a good story to tell her when we first met. How instead of me falling flat on my face she fell on hers before seeing me for the first time. I reached down and picked up the photograph, preparing myself for the big moment. The flip, my future here in my hands.

I could've cried when there was nothing but black in front of my eyes. I thought it was a mistake perhaps, and fished around in the envelope for the documentation. There it was, in large, block letters, two very unfriendly words. NO MATCH greeted me on cream stationary, and underneath the two words in light blue link was the signature of Harrison Ryerson, rushed as if he had to get somewhere in a hurry.

I continued to stare at the paper and the blackness of the photograph, my eyes switching between the two, helplessly hoping that it was all a mistake. But I knew, how could I not? My name on the envelope, the cream paper. The last four numbers of my credit card on the receipt, all neat and settled. This was for me, and it was nothing but the emptiness I carried with me to work, to home, to the bar each Friday, Saturday, and Sunday night. This was proof of the emptiness, something I had to pay to get. I could've cried, could've broken down, but I didn't. I felt a calmness wash over me, and as I plopped my wallet next to my keys, I let out a sigh that replaced the yelp of joy I'd only had moments before. What a world I'd created for myself, to even be rejected by the one company guaranteed to find your SoulMate.

I could've cried but all I could do, and all I can do now, is say I'm stubborn, say I'm bitter, and maybe even throw in a line about how it still isn't right for a dating company to have unrequited access to government records. LT is a wonderful company for 60% of the United States, and soon possibly the world, but that won't stop me for going to the bar on Friday after work and crossing my fingers when I stop staring into the depths of the beer in my glass and look across past the barkeep to the woman whose eyes I'll catch that she hasn't already picked up her Wednesday mail. Life's too short to worry about the black emptiness a picture can give you. The morning will always come, and I'll be there to greet it each and every morning I can.

And maybe someday there will be someone to greet it with me. We might hate each other one moment and like each other's company the next. Love doesn't have to be bought. Love can be fought for, can be squeezed, can be screamed at, can be shoved again and again and again into the emptiness until one day the cream of the paper won't hold the words NO MATCH and the photograph won't be black and the world won't be so empty anymore.

Love conquers all, and one day it will conquer me. For now I'll wait, my mailbox empty, my coffee black, and my life no longer the same. Each day is a new beginning, and each night I know my match can't be bought, because they don't exist. I just have to go out on Friday night, tired from work but heart willing, and catch a glimpse from the girl on the other side of the bar. Who knows, happiness might be waiting for me to buy her a drink.

LIKE HIM

"Your title?"

"Name or, like, what I do for work?"

"Both, if you like, but I only need the name."

"Full or-?"

"Full will do the trick."

"Is this, is that going to be one of the three questions? I heard there's only three questions, and my wife, she said the Peterson's are coming over at six or so."

"You're married?"

"Well, yeah, I mean, that's the point of all of this, isn't it?"

"Just didn't expect that from your replies."

"Was that the second question?"

"If you knew you had dinner why didn't you call and change the appointment like we offer?"

"She sprung the dinner on me or maybe I forgot, I don't know. But that's why I'm here, right? Can't focus any more, can't keep on going."

"Right, right, right, easy now. We're almost ready."

"So those weren't the questions?"

"I try to get to know who I'm dealing with before we start. An intro, if anything."

"The whole success of LifeTime relies solely on the fact that you should already know who I am. You've got my profile right there."

"Right, well,can't blame me for trying."

"My wife can."

"Can't argue that. Let's get going, shall we?"

"She's gonna kill me if I'm late."

"After this is over, you won't even know she exists."

Flick the lighter once, twice, three times. Hover my hand over the flame, that beautiful tint of orange crisping my palm. I'm not a smoker, never have been, but I keep one or two handy. Never know when a customer might need a smoke, especially after I'm done with 'em. Not every day you find your life turned upside down after three simple questions.

The man I just finished up with tonight carries the title of Ben Pitford. He works at a local car dealership down the road, so I told him it'd be easier for me to come to him then for him to try and make it downtown at 6:30 in the evening. Ben is a good looking, mid-forties type. Probably had been working the car game for longer than I've been doing the matching joint. Probably had more than just a wife waiting for him to come home to dinner at eight with the Petersons from next door. I won't tell them that what they are doing is wrong because I wouldn't have my job. Who am I judge anyhow? I'm just the guy helping them find their SoulMate.

I used to work as a recruiter for a local college in Southern California. Travelled a whole bunch, made my name and calling the same. You have a kid who's a sophomore in high school? They probably know me. A junior? They've definitely picked up one of my viewbooks. Heaven help you if you've got a senior, they probably shook my hand and told me how eager they were to attend my institution. What they didn't know was I didn't set foot on the campus until they were home for the summer, out of class and school out of their head. Instead I just kept on roaming, the next fair or the next school a drive, a flight, a walk down the road. At least until LT knocked on my door.

"Must feel strange, right? The recruiter being recruited?"

"I've had my share."

"Confidence, we like that."

"I wouldn't say I've got it, just know what not to say really."

"Well, that isn't too shabby either. Now, have you heard about us before? About what we do?"

"I deserve more, right? Or is it love?"

"Ah, our marketing department finds another. I'll have to tell them of their success when I head back home."

"Does it really, I mean you really think it works?"

"Listen, if I didn't work for LifeTime, I'd already be one of its followers. It's for real."

"But how? Doesn't make sense, just matching up through a website. Doesn't mean it's perfect, like you say it is."

"That's where we are different. It doesn't just take a click and a conversation. We have an algorithm that we use, developed by our creator."

"You're telling me an algorithm does the trick?"

"And our recruiters of course. If you were to join our family, you'd understand why. We'd train you through a month program, really great stuff actually-"

"Right, right, right, I get training. How are the recruiters that important?"

"Because they see who we are working with right away. All the website does is take their credit card information and make them fill out a profile. The recruiters come to help, well help dreams come true."

"So you're saying I wouldn't have to travel? Stay in my territory?"

"Would that be a good thing?"

"Wouldn't hurt, I guess."

You make sure the duffel doesn't weigh over fifty pounds when you first start out in the game of college recruiting. They tell you other things, like make sure you always smile, always stand at the fairs, always put out your best, but the number one piece you've got to take into consideration is to make damn sure that the duffel isn't over fifty pounds. The airline you travel on for the college will charge you extra if it's over fifty, and you don't want any of that fresh, terrible noise. You make sure the duffel is under fifty by separating what you really need from what you want, just like every other situation you'll encounter in this life.

You may think you need seventy-four pamphlets for the fair in downtown Atlanta that night, but you know it's only going to take forty-five since you're college is in Southern California and not the South. You'd like to believe the kids running around the fair are there for the schools, to learn a little bit more about what college might be like, but you know all they want is that shiny looking pen you're hawking at your table in exchange for what you want, which is their fingers wrapping around it to fill out an information card on who they are, what they want to study, and why they might choose your institution as a possibility for their future. Numbers, it's always about the numbers.

Once you got the duffel game solved you should be set, right? The college will train you well in what they expect, what numbers to hit, and it helps that you attended the place for four years of your life. The best four years you think when they hand you a nametag with the year you graduated underneath your name. The past always looks brighter when you step further and further away from it.

Hotels are nice in the fall, havens in the winter, and horrid in the summer. Spring is spring, and in parts of the country you can roll down your window as you trek for the hour to another school on your list and smell the seasons all around you. It's a funny feeling doing so much travelling for a job. You never know when you're going to land and find home again.

"What's the pay like?"

"Salary of course. Looking at eighty to ninety a year, plus benefits."

"You know I'm in education, right? That's an insane amount of money."

"Well, we've read up on you. Asked the right people the right questions. We like what we've been hearing."

"What would be the territory?"

"Nothing out West, so you'd have to move. We'd pay for everything obviously, once you found a place."

"Where would it be?"

"We're looking to expand our brand even further, which you were probably already aware of before we sat down. You're young, which is a plus for us. Many of our clients don't like seeing an elder statesmen tell them about love. They want someone younger, makes it more believable."

"As if all we're doing is dreaming, right?"

"Isn't that what love is all about?"

"Seems like a jump. I'm pretty cautious these days."

"We're not going anywhere anytime soon. You'll be in safe hands if you decide to join the LT family, I can promise you that."

"Right, right, right. You, ah, you've got my ear. I give two weeks today over the phone, what happens next?"

"We fly you to D.C. to for a month. Put you up in a one bedroom apartment, stock the fridge, give you the time to process and understand the purpose of the job, rather than just the work you'll be doing. Then we send you off to Memphis, find you a home, probably in Germantown, and you begin."

"Tennessee? Interesting."

"Fun town, real good place to be. Smacks you right in the middle of where we need you. You'll be doing mostly driving, maybe the occasional flight. LT has already conquered the coasts, now is the time to take the rest of the country by storm."

"You talk like we're in a war."

"Not necessarily. A fight, a battle, but not a war. War was over when Harrison Ryerson got the go ahead to launch LifeTime. We're just cleaning up the pieces one by one, and taking the next step when we feel it's the right time."

"Sound like you've got it together."

"You could say that. It seems like we're dancing around the words that you want to say though, aren't we? It's not too difficult to embrace the change, embrace the idea. A blind man could see what's all over your face right now, can't hid that at all. Should I slide the offer sheet over to you, or do you want to grab it out of my hands yourself?"

D.C. is a tourist town when you get right down to it. I know I'm probably stating the obvious, but with the most powerful man in the world holding court a couple hundred yards away from LifeTime's HQ you'd think it'd be worth more than folks buying trinkets and pictures of themselves in front of statues and landmarks. LT had it together, much more than I thought at the time. I assumed they were a good start-up, considering the money they promised. Cost of living alone in Memphis guaranteed me a nice paycheck from them each month. Crazy how quickly life can change but that was the point, wasn't it? Just like their company their offer seemed too good to be true.

Even now as Ben Pitford walks to his car, shaking his head before dropping his keys on the ground, I can't think that what I'm doing is reality. The training in D.C. was similar to the college in so many ways it made me think that maybe LT was just another institution cranking up their own college beginning. As a national recruiter for LifeTime my job was simple.

I met the client after we had a phone conversation, the talk typically right after they finished up the payment portion of the exercise and received the picture and information. LT's stat nerds did numbers on this, and wouldn't you know that even at three in the morning I'd hear the buzz on my nightstand of another life found, the shaky voice on the other end secretly hoping I wasn't real. The boogeyman of love, was that okay to say? A nightmare turned reality, and these clients, they were special because they couldn't handle what they purchased. I talked them into the impossible. My job was to recruit them into LT's bosom and make them see the light. I sold them on leaving everything they had for a dream we created.

In a normal session the client selects the location, since they know the territory better. They'll dial the 800 number and, based on their location, their call will redirect to the recruiter for the region. Upon hearing the answer I quickly research how far it would take me to drive, fly or, if lucky, walk to the client from my current location. This time was lucky, as Ben happened to live in Germantown, which is basically Memphis but without the crippling poverty right on your doorstep. Upon hearing Ben mention he was in Germantown I knew I was in luck, and told him that I was getting on a plane immediately and would arrive at noon at the front of the Graceland Museum entrance the next day. You always tell the client that you are flying to create the illusion that yes, we're all in D.C., New York, Los Angeles.

LifeTime may help you find everlasting happiness with your SoulMate, a very family friendly idea in one light, but that doesn't mean we aren't trendy, we aren't important, we aren't worth your time. The coasts are what matters to a company's image, the rest of the country important to the budget, or more importantly each and every executive's wallet.

The next day around eleven thirty I hop into my car and make my way to Graceland. Most of the recruiters probably wouldn't like the noise that Graceland represents but then again I didn't belong with them anyhow. LT had wanted me for a reason, a need, and I was supplying them beautifully. Our numbers had gone higher and higher in the South in general, but Tennessee was skyrocketing. My boss didn't have to tell me I was doing a great job because I could see it in every face I met.

"Funny that you picked here, you know that right?"

"Figured it was a landmark that would be pretty easy. You don't mind the recorder, do you?"

"Is that how this all works?"

"You could question it, be late for dinner."

"Fucking dinner. You're right, I paid for this, I need to relax. Are we just going to walk around, or-?"

"We'll go outside and sit on one of the benches near the restaurant in just a moment. From there I'll ask you two of the three questions. After the second question is answered we'll head out to the parking lot, I'll ask the third and then you'll be on your way in time for dinner with the Peterson's. It'll go as smoothly as you want it to."

"We couldn't have just done this at a park? Or, I don't know, anywhere else in Memphis?"

"I like the tackiness of it all. Also, you can always find love at

25

Graceland, right?"

"That doesn't make sense. Are you really part of LT?"

"Of course I am, but I'm more fun than the others. Love is supposed to be fun, right? Now let's head for the tables, the place closes in thirty minutes."

The recruiter and the client must always be face to face for the session to commence, eyes wide open and staring. They teach you this at the facility in Washington. They grind it into your head, they grind it into your genes. You can't allow for the client to face away, or close his eyes, or ask if they can write it down on a scrap of paper. You've got to have their full attention, because without the right answers they won't buy into the product, they won't buy into what we sold them. You calmly sit down, smile, and ask the first question, then hold up the recorder right under their nose to make sure you get the answer. They'll smile at first when they hear it, because they think you're joking.

"You comfortable Ben?"

"I don't know if I want you using my real name. How about, I don't know, Tom?"

"Ben, we know it's you. I know it's you. Don't be silly, remember, this goes as smoothly as you want it to."

"Okay, sorry, I, well I don't know. Just didn't feel right."

"Right never left when you clicked accept payment on LT's website. You're here to find your way, and it is the correct way. Are you ready for the first question?"

"Shoot."

"Why are you here?"

"You're kidding."

"Is that the answer you want to give?"

"No that's not the answer I want to give, but is that really the question? Why am I here? Because you chose fucking Graceland, a tourist spot, as a meeting place. I thought you were fucked in the head when you said that, but I thought, oh he's from out of town, he probably doesn't know better. So I gave you the benefit of the doubt, and now I get this?"

"Ben you need to focus on the question if you want this to go anywhere."

"Fucking kidding me with this crap, you've got to be shitting me. Okay, why am I here, you want to know why? Because I thought it was a gimmick, a stupid game."

"That it? That's the answer you want to give?"

"No, I'm still thinking. Fuck it, why I am here? I'm here because I'm unhappy."

"Unhappy with what exactly?"

"Is that the second question?"

"No Ben, I'll tell you. Why are you unhappy, Ben?"

"I'm unhappy because I'm not with my SoulMate, is that what you want to hear? Shit, forty bucks might not be it, but what am I doing, right? God, everything is the same, each and every day. I'm unhappy because I'm stuck in Germantown, Tennessee with a woman and a family I didn't want. I'm unhappy because I want to move to a different town, a different place, and not have to take on the responsibility of a life that shouldn't be mine in the first place."

"That's good Ben, that's great."

"Glad you enjoyed it. Someone has to."

"These questions aren't meant to be difficult, because you'll know the answer before I ask them. It's important to be truthful during this session, not just for your results but for your mind. I'm going to ask the second question now, are you ready?"

"Sure."

"What does it mean to be in a relationship?"

"What does it mean to be in a relationship? Good question."

"You need to speak impulsively, not think through the question but say what first comes to mind."

"I get it, I know. What does it mean to be in a relationship? I think it means I found the person I want to spend time with, the person I want to see when I need someone most. Doesn't have to be physical, needs to be intimate. Needs to mean more than just an affair. I keep on thinking, hoping, that my wife and I will work it out. Keep on doing the pro and con lists in my head over and over. She moved here because of me you know. I grew up here, went away to college and when I needed to come back for my family, for my mom, my dad, she followed me. She stuck with me all the way. So I make the lists in my head, add that to the pro column. I keep on going back and forth all the time, but when I get home each night from work, when I see her face look away from the television at mine, I just don't have the spark that means I need her. I don't need her the most anymore, and I don't know how to explain it. I question all the time if I ever really needed her, or if I filled my head up with thoughts to make me believe I did. Does that, does that make sense?"

The walk back to the parking lot is always the worst but you never tell the client that. You're part of a bigger entity, part of a larger idea. You are LifeTime as a recruiter, whether you are in Las Vegas standing in front of a drive-thru chapel or in Alaska wondering how fate guided you to the small town of Skagway, let out by a biplane because a client with worries popped up overnight. You represent a future that is brighter than the client can even imagine, and though the walk is terrible there is meaning behind it. Ben Pitford opened up not once but twice when the recorder was shoved under his nose. Now he's about to breakdown, drop his keys on the ground in only a few minutes and tell himself that dinner with the Peterson's isn't worth a single dime. You'll walk over after the recorder is turned off, smile a weak smile and pick him up, dust his back off and right the ship. You're a recruiter, you're human. You're just like him.

"You've got your wallet, your keys?"

"I do, right here."

"After this last question the session will be over. You will return home and not worry anymore, okay? We provide a service, and though it may seem complicated you will embrace it. You've chosen LT for a reason, Ben, and you will embrace this reason and this path. Do you understand this?"

"I do."

"You're doing great, Ben. I hope you know that."

"Just ask the question already."

"Right, right, right, let's not delay. I'm going to ask the third and final question now, are you ready?"

"I am."

"Okay, here we go. What do you believe being in love is?"

"I, well, I don't know exactly. I don't think I've ever experienced it, to tell you the truth. I think maybe with my, well, my first girlfriend, I could tell you I felt it then. That feeling in your stomach, you know the one. Like it disappeared on you all of a sudden, and you're left with this hole that needs to be filled. People call it butterflies and I think that might be an okay explanation, but then again it just isn't. Being in love is when you look into that person's eyes and see more than just a relationship. You see your life in their eyes, right in their eyes. You see everything you can become when they smile, you see everything you want to be when they walk by you in the morning. You have a feeling that you deserve more, but you're not sure when they walk in. You get flustered, your heartbeat soars. Love is your body shutting down and giving way to another, more meaningful way of living. You die the moment you find the one you want to be with forever, because you think you're eternally dreaming. You die, and you never wake up. I guess that sounds pretty corny coming from the mouth of a car salesman, but then again who says I'm meant to sell cars anymore? Who says I'm meant for anything except finding the one I want to be with, the one I'm meant to be with."

Ben Pitford will make it home to dinner on time and act the same way he has all through the night. He'll know what's coming, and when he gets the nerve he'll sit down with his wife in front of the television and tell her. His life has already changed when he turns the engine on and drives away from the Graceland parking lot, leaving me next to my car with the recorder in my hands, my pulse quick and my breath heavy. He's gone now, a new man, a new SoulMate.

I don't know if I should've left the college game, and it's something I look back on every day with every new dissatisfied client passing my way. LT has a vision that I appreciate it, and I know that what I do is right in some circles. In others it isn't, and that's the ones I hold onto. I pretend to believe I know where each of my steps will land next, but all I can do is wonder if all this is really worth the happiness, or more an easy path for the pain?

When I begin to mix my emotions with my job, when I think that I should leave and walk far, far away, my phone buzzes in my pocket. Another call, another client, another stat, another day. I get into my car, slide to answer, my new voice for this client, this person, about to turn into a fresh beginning.

The Graceland parking lot becomes a blip on the horizon as I talk to Mrs. Annie Young, a blip in my mind, a blip in my past. We're discussing location, timing, the next step. I tell her only one thing before I hang up the phone, shift my car into drive and leave

Memphis to head for my next stop, Springfield, Missouri. Your next step, regardless of what you may believe, of what you may think, will always be the justifiably right one, because only you are taking it .

MORE ROLLS, LESS SASHIMI

"Hold up, I think I forgot my keys in the car."

"You mean the keys that you put in your coat pocket?"

"Right…well…I mean, it was worth a shot."

"That's what you think, but I'm going to tell your future wife about this little ruse and she's going to be very, very upset with you."

"If I meet her today."

"That's why we're here, you'll meet her. They guarantee it."

I didn't just arrive here, if that's what you're thinking. You might see me from a distance laughing with George and think, "Wow, those two guys are hitting it off, maybe this is just another one of those tech conventions I keep hearing about." You'd be wrong about the convention, and about George and me hitting it off. We've known each other for four years, ever since we first heard about the whole online dating agency profession. George and I are, I guess, veterans of the industry.

Ever since LT was introduced a couple of movements ceased their existence. I'm talking about the dating sites, the agencies which really didn't have a specific purpose. You know the ones I'm talking about of course, so why re-hash any silly plot points of our story and instead focus on why I'm standing with George outside of the NRG Center in Houston twiddling my thumbs and hoping for a flash flood to hit our location. I don't have a boat like Noah did but I do have a car which I can sit on top of for an hour before I drown. It'd be nicer than actually having to walk inside and work the convention.

You'll notice my attention span kind of…drifts off into the great unknown from time to time. I'll take an idea and run with it for a good minute or so, then leapfrog that idea and move onto the next one, the cycle going on and on and on until I'm bored or tired. When that happens you'll finally have the chance to break the silence and ask, "But what about when we first started talking? What about that idea, Frank?" and I'll be off again on another pointless tangent.

LifeTime's greatest victory was when they started being proven correct on their "love judgements", as we like to call them from the outside. LT wasn't going to get anywhere by being just another pay-to-date website. I mean, the name is catchy enough, I guess, but nothing to build an empire from.

When their love judgements ended up hitting, when the couples stayed together and found what they really believed were their SoulMates, well, that just blew the company to where it is now. Sitting so far up in the clouds they probably think they are alone and, in a way, they are. Save for the specialized dating pools of course.

That's where yours truly comes into play, which you might've figured out by now. When the plain Jane websites pulled their plugs ours stayed firm. LT knows they'll be fine in a world where they and us both exist, because they've got their believers and we've got ours. Ours are just so much older in origin, our believers having that faith you can't find by seeing your SoulMate on a photograph from the mail.

Typically I work the religious conventions George and I are opening the doors to now, my keys in my coat pocket and my heart in my throat, the beat-beat-beat reverberating through my person. Dating within your faith is just practical, because not only do you push the faith forward but you've got the most important thing you can have already in common. LifeTime won't steal away the Christians, the Mormons, the Buddhists even, though I could see it. Harrison Ryerson even mentioned it when LT first went over a billion in worth. "Not worth the fight" he said, half-smiling at the cameras or maybe to himself. He knew a battle was over before a gun was drawn. Man was intelligent, unlike George and me.

There is that saying, I think it goes "don't shit where you eat", right? What George and I were doing was exactly what the saying said not to do, and we were doing it for not only a fee but with a smile on our idiotic faces. All because George and I knew the woman running it.

Before we get any further let me lay out what George and I are representing today, and why I don't want to be here. George doesn't know the reason because I haven't told him the reason yet, and I probably, more than likely will never speak a lick to him about the reason. Maybe when I'm able to quit the race, move out to the country somewhere in West Texas, where the day moves slower.

George is part of the Houston Catholic Brigade, or the HCB, which focuses its attention on the forty to forty-nine age group of men and women hoping to find the love of their life, outside of their Lord and Savior of course. He's twenty-eight, slightly out of shape and likes to keep a thin mustache above his upper lip because he thinks it makes him look mysterious and, therefore, a conversation starter at the conventions he works. His boss will be here today and when she's sees him she'll will run over and try to cover up his face. That, or shave it off with a razor.

George's name tag is already stamped over his heart on the lime green polo he decided to wear to where we are today, the tenth annual Faith + Love Festival, and I can't keep shaking my head at its ridiculousness. His name printed out, and below that his faith in bright red.

"I don't know why they always have to put the Catholics in red. Doesn't give off the best vibe, right?"

"It's the blood, man, it's the blood thing. You know all you people are."

"All us people? Frank, that's not cool. You sure you didn't forget your manners in the car with your keys?"

"Ha, now that'll hit well with the singles here."

"I feel kind of guilty being here, Frank. Like we're shooting fish in a barrel."

"A really big barrel George. A barrel big enough that some fish won't care about getting shot."

George thinks wearing lime green shows comfortability with himself, especially if he doesn't sweat through the shirt. I, on the other hand, have gone with a classic white, long sleeved button-up and a skinny black tie because, as I told George the night before, "I want to look like I belong in front of the booth, and not behind it." Difficult, acting as if you should be in a certain place, especially one you've worked before. Loneliness will do that to a man though.

You've probably realized at this point a couple of key facts I've let go missing, and don't worry, I'll come back to them now. First, why I'm so unhappy to be here. Yeah, the whole finding love where I work aspect of Faith + Love doesn't really help my mood, but I can get over it eventually. It won't be fun seeing my co-workers, and they'll wonder what in the heck I'm doing with the fish, but that's not too much to get worked up over. I might even look back and laugh when it's all done. It'll be easier to do when I found the woman I'm going to spend the rest of my life with today.

These festivals are really great to work, and I'll tell you why: you get to see love evolve over a couple of hours, and what happens is you really start believing in what you do. LifeTime acts like they know what love really means, and on some level they probably do. But what we have here, seeing people find love through love, through faith, it's actually quite amazing. George thinks I'm a crabby guy, that I don't get the whole point of the festivals but deep down, when the lights shut down and we walk out after a five-hour stint behind our booths, I actually take a deep breath and smile, even though George will never know. He's a Catholic male who wasn't married at twenty-two, he's got enough to worry about after the work is done for the day.

Attending these festivals on the other hand is terrifying, and I will once again tell you why: because the schmucks behind the booth actually believe in what they are selling to the fish and today, Lord help me, I'm one of that endless barrel. You've got me, a twenty-seven year old male with a beer belly and a laugh that frightens small children, and I'm expected to go home with a woman, an actual person who wants to spend the rest of their life with me? George jokes the women have already found the One they really want to be with so having a fool like me as their second isn't the end of the world. He likes to tell me as much as possible how easy we'll have it today, but I'm not buying.

"Besides Frank, you've got some decent moving strength, right? I bet you could help move any number of cabinets if she asked you to. You're one heck of a living room arranger, and one lucky woman is going to have you moving coffee tables three inches to the right with ease for the rest of her life."

"George, my name tag keeps falling off. What are these made of?"

"Just hold it up like a passport or something."

"A passport? As if I won't be embarrassed enough walking through the open doors in a few minutes."

"Where we meeting after we're done, Frank?"

"I thought you said we'd be through after this."

"You know that's not how it works, plus you're my ride."

"Right, George, I'm just messing around. Let's, ah, let's end up here before we head home."

"Good luck man, keep that name tag high!"

"You too, George, good luck man."

"It's going to be fine, remember, you're Frank Cohen, and you've got what they're looking for."

Faith + Love makes sure to separate the different religions in different wings of the NRG Center. You might think this would cause a bit of space issue for those religions that draw a lot or a handful but right there you would be wrong. These things always just draw everybody in the area, and there's a reason they only host them in big cities like Houston. This Faith + Love is built around not only the Houston territory but the entirety of Texas.

Think about that for a moment, really think about it, and then think about how on my one day off from this week long festival I decided to come with my Catholic friend on "You've Found Faith, Now Find Love" Day, the busiest, craziest, most ridiculous day of the entire thing.

If you're still with me, and I'm guessing you are, you've probably realized this is one of those festivals, those events that really does cram you in like sardines in a can. I may be lucky to just find my own group's booth in Wing J, which is where I'm standing outside of now.

Faith + Love started out small, just like LifeTime, but now they're both too big to understand and folks like me only come because they already knew about it or, if they're desperate enough, to find if it's really worth climbing through to find your spouse. What's worse about my situation is I'm not like George, who really knows what he's looking for in a partner. George is new to the game, a fresh face that loves working for the HCB and simply decided now is the time for a change. He's never dated anyone for more than a week, never felt a connection. He'll be the king of the barrel in about an hour I'd reckon, even his own booth hyping him up for the other fish. Myself on the other hand, well…that's a bit more complicated, not that my booth wouldn't be doing for me what George's will for him. Just that I'm not sure if I'm really ready for everything at this moment.

There's already a line out front, maybe two to three hundred people. A small huddle of giggling women, mid-thirties I'd say, turn their eyes to stare at me, clucking away. Do I want an older wife? Not sure, but the way the one with black hair and the fake, turquoise rimmed glasses stares at me I'm considering going over and giving it a conversational try. It's not too difficult to believe but these conventions really go like a high school dance. When the doors open there will be rows of booths with different faith-based groups at each booth, and every single person will have to decide which group they want to dance with, so to speak. Just like your faith the booths depend on who you are, what you want to look for, and, most important of all, where you feel like you can find your future.

As if they've shot the starting pistol, right? That's the saying, no? Maybe it's starter, I'm not entirely sure, but you know what I'm getting at, don't you? It's the start of the race, the moment when the sprinters actually start doing what they are named for. That moment, that time is exactly how it feels when they finally give the groups the go ahead to venture forth into the wings, and if you aren't ready at your booth you might as well pack it up and walk out, because it's going to move quicker than you ever anticipated.
Not hard to imagine really but behind me waits another teeming mass of potential partners, men and women like myself who are ready to mingle amongst the booths.

I walk in next to a shorter fellow who keeps on spraying mouth freshener on his tongue while he takes each step. I shake my head, grinning. The thrill of swimming upstream is much more exciting than I thought possible. I've always been staring at the mass, not a member of it. Never thought I would, considering where I was only a handful of years ago. But that's for another time.

You've got your booths separated by age at the front, which is important. What's really practical about LifeTime is they do find the exact person you're intended to be with, which in our industry we laugh at because it is the lazy way out. No work needed, right to your mailbox SoulMate access. However, if you are looking at Faith + Love just for someone with your faith and in your age range, it's nice to only walk a few steps and possibly have access. Eighteen-nineteen is right at the entrance, the youth draw big for these events. Sometimes, if they know beforehand, they'll rent out an entire theatre or a staging space for these age groups, based of course on population turnout.

You've got the twenties, the thirties, the forties, so on and so forth following after the teens. The men and women that drift toward ages younger than theirs tend to be turned away based on principle, but sometimes if a flash of green occurs you might see them brought into a booth for matching. A basis of faith, of religion, is to be able to procreate and bring more into the fold, and a seventy-five year old woman looking for a thirty-three year old man may not be the best pairing to have a child.

The age-based groups are tiresome because they usually get the most foot-traffic. It's easy to match when all you have is faith and age, and for some that's really all they are looking for. There's nothing wrong with going the easy route, especially if you are older and don't want to go through the hassle, the work required by other booths here today. You've got the Lord, you've got twenty or so years left, and you wouldn't mind having someone by your side with the exact same qualities.

I, on the other hand, don't have the time for the age-group booths, not just because nearly half the crowd has already descended upon them but because, as George said, I'm looking for my wife today, and I'd like to believe we have more than just faith and our time on this planet in common.

Two rows of booths greet me when I walk into Wing J, and as I shuffle down the first row of age-based groups and turn left into the next row I prepare to try and not be seen by the group I work for. They'll be right near that first turn into the second row, and maybe if I crouch down a ways I could—

"Frank? Frank, is that you? Frank, you know it's your day off, right?"

"Hey Paul, Diane, how's it going?"

"Frank, I don't want to alarm you but there's some kind of weird fabric wrapped around your neck that's trying to kill you."

"Diane, don't waste that one on me, save it for the rest of these folks."

"Frank, are you looking here? Diane, I told you he was looking. Frank, we can do a profile for you, you know. It would make sense, since you work here."

"I appreciate it Paul, I really do, but I want to try a different route. On my own, you know?"

"You're going to make us cry, this is just...we didn't expect this."

"Has been a while champ, so to say Diane and I aren't happy for you would be a lie."

"Well I mean, I don't know if it'll happen here, but I thought—"

"Oh Frank, it'll happen, don't you worry about that. You're going to find her, I guarantee it."

"Get that in writing?"

"Frank, move along and get going. Don't waste your time here, go find the right fit."

"Ouch, Diane, didn't think I'd hear that from you."

"You just be you. Remember, we love you for more than what you wear, though you look nice. Just be you and it'll all work out."

Paul and Diane are married with two kids named Tyler and Ted, but he goes by Teddy now since he got tired of writing three letters instead of five. They started Faith & Fun in response to LT not having the components they found in each other, just like most of the independents here. I started working for them because of their message and, more important, because I needed the work and they pay very well. Faith & Fun is definitely a broad name but what Paul and Diane focus their group on is putting together group-dates rather than one-on-ones, using the information they detailed at events like these into putting together a group full of individuals looking for a more low-key first date scenario.

Each group had its matches already laid out on paper of course, but it made for an evening of fun and adventure for the future couples. Based on interests Paul and Diane would set up bowling battles, worship events, or family-style game nights. The reason it all was so going well, why the business was booming so to speak, was because the younger generation, the teens to the twenties, were moving from the age booths to theirs right away and creating a profile. My role in the company was more the traveling face, the compiler of profiles, and the handing out of business cards, which is what why Paul and Diane had to work my day off.

Once you walk past my employer you'll see the second row of booths, and this is where the complications pile up. So many different types of faith-based dating services, so little time. Like ultimate Frisbee and NASCAR? Disc Drive might be your best bet. How about canoeing while discussing presidential candidate's foreign policies? Paddle Politics was here and the rep at the booth, Tony, would not only help you create a profile but teach you the right techniques on the river for an extra ten bucks.

Over seventy-five different independents had booths here today, and since this was the busiest day on the schedule, and for some reason my day off, I was lucky enough to stand in the middle of them all and watch as fish started swimming to each of them in a row. They would listen politely to the pitch, hear about what was so great, so different, so distinct, and then maybe they would stay.

If the fish already knew of the company but had just been waiting for the right opportunity to make a profile in person you might see them run right to a booth, arms waving high and the person behind the booth grinning from ear-to-ear. Of course you could set a profile up online, every booth here had a website, but there was something special about possibly meeting your spouse in person the moment you completed a profile. Could happen, but usually you had to go through a date first.

A little more about me for a change, since all you've heard is about Wing J, about my beer belly and obnoxious laugh and, most important of all, exactly what George and I are wearing to Faith + Love, at least our top halves anyways. I don't want to spoil anything about the bottom, but I will say I'm wearing navy –stained blue jeans and black tennis shoes. I can't tell you what George wears, only because you know, it's just so fun to imagine what he was willing to wear with the lime green polo.

I would say I stumbled into religion, because where I'm at now is truly where I wasn't meant to be. Do we ever get to actually choose our path, or are we simply pushed along until we decide enough is enough? I had decided enough is enough today of all days, and maybe I'll find my wife. Or maybe I'll just design a profile that gets picked up two months later, when I'm already gone and in Portland, Oregon for another convention, this time behind the booth, safe and secure.

Swimming with the fish is fun, but when you've felt love before coming to the NRG Center and making sure your name tag is correct, well, it makes it a bit more difficult to swallow. If I'm caught staring too long in the mirror before, it's not because I'm nervous about what the others will think, it's because I'm trying to piece together what I'm actually looking at. A man, in my eyes, is someone who can make their own while keeping their own, and I've already lost the latter. I would call my ex my own, only because I thought we were similar. I thought we had what was needed, what life is all about.

She was shorter than me and when I wasn't leaning down to kiss her she would get on her tip-toes, grab my shoulders and give me a quick peck on the cheek to get my attention before spinning around and asking if she had anything stuck to her back, her skirt picking up slightly when she spun and my eyes drifting to her lower half and then back to her mischievous eyes once I realized all she wanted was for me to stare at her the way I tended to do.

We were right there at the edge of marriage, the last step so close and yet obviously so far away. When she left she took my heart for a while and I took her religion for longer, the pair of us not wanting to move on even as we drifted further and further apart. Sometimes I think I'll see her at one of these things, smiling with her brand new husband on her arm. I don't know what I'll do if it actually happens, but I'd like to think it would go well. Frank Cohen, a nice guy, what a concept. George, Paul, and Diane would all think I went insane.

The noise level of Wing J has just gotten out of control now, and I'm starting to feel the squeeze of the barrel around me. I'm staring now, gazing off in the direction of the end of the second row. Truthfully I don't know what I want, or what I'm expecting out of this today. I hear the celebratory squeals of people finding their group, their booth, and I smile because it's nice when folks find happiness in the simplest of things. I just don't want people thinking I'm too obnoxious or too bitter, that's all. I come off a certain way that rubs people wrong sometimes, but for the most part I really help sell Faith & Fun like I've already found both. I guess that's why Paul and Diane are happy for me today, of all days. They know I'll find the glint in my eye instead of that false, dead stare I carry now.

There's a booth third from the end on the left side of the second row that doesn't have a single soul at it, just sitting empty handed with nothing going for it. I hate the loneliness, hate the empty silence you get when that happens, and decide to swim forward to see if it's something I'd sign up for.

"You do what now?"

"We match creative individuals together in faith. Kind of like a one-stop source for artists who believe in God."

"Artists? Like professionals?"

"Not necessarily, more like people who just continue on with the possibility of professionalism."

"I, uh, I like that. I like that a lot. How come you aren't at these more often?"

"We actually just started up only a few months ago. We were too small for the circuit until now, but don't worry, we're growing at a very high rate."

"Don't worry about the growth, it'll come. I work for Faith & Fun, down at the end of the block."

"Oh, oh wow, so you're that Frank Cohen."

"Guess I'm pretty easy to spot at my booth, right?"

"But you are unique, I've heard about Frank Cohen from Faith & Fun since we arrived. And you're looking at us for a profile, no?"

"I mean, why not. If you'll have me, of course?"

"Before we officially draw up a profile and talk a fee, we always make sure to ask our clients what their creative outlet is."

"Right, that makes sense. I like to, uh, I like to write stories on the side. Nothing special, but I kept it up from when I was in college."

"So you'll be classified as a writer on your profile, is that okay for you?"

"Ha, I guess it is. Never thought of myself as a writer outside of daydreams."

"I'm happy to help you Frank. My name is Clarence, and welcome to Creativity with Christ."

"I wanted to ask, when will I hear back after we go through the profile? Like, what's the next step?"

"Well Frank, once we compile your profile today and go through security checks to make sure you are a Creativity with Christ candidate, we will send you a name, time, and address where you're first date will be."

"Kind of LifeTime-y, isn't it?"

"Well sometimes you have to borrow from the best, even if it is something little. Are you ready to begin? I've got the paperwork we can fill out right here."

"I guess I am. I don't...well I don't usually do this so quickly."

"Frank, I want you to stop and take a breath. Pause for a moment, Frank."

"Um…okay."

"Frank, you've worked these so you are no doubt aware the type of people who walk in the aisle behind you now. They are looking for something that LT cannot provide. They are looking for a real connection beyond just the simplicity of being told about their SoulMate. They want the experience of recognizing a spirit within a soul. You know this, right Frank?"

"I, I do. I guess I never looked at it that way before."

"You seem ready, Frank. But I do want to promise you one thing Frank, and that is you will find your partner with us. We need faith, but what Creativity with Christ provides is a chance for you to explore beyond our faith and beyond the basics. You share a desire that's not just physical, not just spiritual. I believe you are ready to find a partner you just don't see your heart through but indeed one you match intellectually, one that drives you to be better."

"Clarence, you really care about your work, don't you?"

"I believe we're doing something special here."

"Well, we all are. Thanks for the speech, really builds a guy up, you know? I'm ready when you are. Or as ready as I will be. Let's find my wife."

Creativity with Christ, now there's a name for you. Clarence wasn't the founder, and from his long-winded explanations I don't know if I wanted to hear the individual's story. Heck, their origin might have been founded by a group, or by God. Formed out of thin air, appearing only to those fortunate enough to discover the booth at one of these conventions, or possibly their website.

I didn't really care, only because the concept sounded intriguing.

George, Paul, Diane, they had all made it clear I was intended to find my partner at this event, so the fact this wife of mine could be someone with an artistic flair, whatever that really meant, was intriguing. Right now though, walking away from a beaming Clarence and out of Wing J and into the lobby some two hours after I arrived, all I could picture was simply another person like me, typing away at their computer in an over-crowded Starbucks, pretending they are a writer.

George is laughing at me when I walk up, holding a handful of papers in his hands. He's laughing because I walk up with one piece and Clarence's business card, my profile smaller than the ones he picked up from Wing D. He begins talking at me, probably mentioning his day or bringing up a quick story he found hilarious, but I'm miles away in my head. Clarity is a funny thing to discuss, to contemplate, but when it really hits your brain, when the clouds drift away and you realize the next step you take is sincere, it means something more, well…it's kind of difficult to focus on your buddy's round at a religious dating convention.

"So this one chick, she comes right up to me and, you aren't going to believe this, mentions how hot I look in the polo."

"This happened just now? Does she know where she is?"

"Frank, I'm not going to lie, I honestly thought she was going to LifeTime me. Her eyes, her tongue, I was convinced I was about to be taken off the market."

"But LT doesn't reach into religious streams, you know that."

"Like they really know who they're pulling half the time. Love Experts be damned, their algorithm wouldn't know if they were pulling a Mormon or Jew. I feel like they just publish they don't because of some kind of religious freedom agreement or something."

"So are you going to marry the crazy? She did say you were hot."

"I thought about it, she had a nice top on. But that's not what I'm

46

looking for."

"Right, and based on the six profiles you filled out you definitely have a grasp on what you're looking for."

"Frank, not all of us can find Creativity with Christ. By the way, you never mentioned you were a writer to me before."

"Well, I mean, I'm not really...but then again, you never asked either."

"Can you write me a poem that I can read to my wife when I meet her? That'd be pretty cool, right?"

"It's your wife, of course it'll be cool. Can it contain roses three to five times?"

"That's romantic Frank, take it easy. I don't want her thinking she snagged too much of a Romeo."

Clarence promised I'd get an email the following Monday with a location, time, and name. He laughed when I said it reminded me of LT but he couldn't deny Creativity definitely borrowed from LifeTime in some ways. Most of the sites did though anyways, there was a reason LT was the number one company for relationship building out there. So what did all of this mean to me? It meant I couldn't focus on anything the entire day. I don't remember brushing my teeth, so just in case I did it three times. Same with the shower, and for all I knew I had two breakfasts and lunches. I wasn't tunnel vision, because that was still too wide. My phone was my friend, and all the way until 4:00 PM I had the television in my apartment on, trying to not stare at the screen waiting for the ding of a message in my inbox.

What's it like seeing the name of the one you're destined for before you see the face? Has to be weird, maybe different. Usually these sites will include a picture so you know what the other person looks like, but Clarence was very adamant when he said I would know. As if our souls would gravitate towards each other or something.

Holly Ryder, the name rolling off my tongue, thrown there over and over and over by my brain. Ryder was a cool last name, would she want to do the hyphen thingy with Cohen because she's an artist? I couldn't see why that would be a problem with me, but my parents might worry I wasn't being husbandly enough. What did it matter anyhow, right? Was I worrying about too much already? I hadn't even met her yet and I was preparing for our first argument, hyping myself up to accept this wasn't going to work out before I had even left the living room in my apartment.

The email says to meet her in front of a sushi joint in downtown Houston, and I wonder if Clarence took my mentioning of "the fish" so many times to be my desire for a raw plate of it. I don't mind sushi, like cut and hand rolls a whole lot, but if Holly wants to do sashimi I'm thinking we might have to pick another spot.

I don't mind the sashimi, but the way it just sits there lonely, a fish literally out of water, when the rolls combine so much together. A roll is a relationship worth taking on, worth diving into. Sashimi is elegant but cold, and though it may taste better than the rolls at first it doesn't have dimensions, doesn't have the layers a roll provides, which is what matters to me. I don't need fancy, I need comfortable. She won't choose sashimi though, that's the point, right? This person matched well with me personality wise, which means it wasn't going to be an issue. We aren't going to be exactly alike but we'll share the core essentials, the foundation. We're humans with similar interests, with similar tastes for the most part.

It's four now, and the dinner is at 6:30 PM. Clarence told me I'd have plenty of time to get ready, but knowing Houston's traffic I probably have about an hour to get going before I should head out the door. What should I wear, nice? Or practical nice? Clarence liked my tie at Faith + Love, should I go with that combo again? What if Holly saw me there and I'm overdoing it, and she thinks I only have one outfit for important times in my life? She'll probably hate that, so I shouldn't…but then again the black tie is a good look. And then you've got my hair, which is just a jerk these days. Sometimes it stays up how I like, other times I look like it just got really windy outside for no reason in particular. Should I go for the product, push my strands out of my eyes and into some kind of fake Elvis? Or just let it flow free, free and easy and let Holly see the real me. Heck, if she wants to see the real me I should probably just show up in a black t-shirt, tan shorts and worn out sandals. It's what she'll see the most of if we end up together, which is the whole point of this, right?

As you can probably guess, I don't do this often, if at all. Dating is difficult, especially when you thought you were done with it so early. At first it's easy to venture out, only because you're in so much pain from the break-up that you don't know the difference between love and lust. That's the rebound, the time to realize not all is hopeless. Three rebounds into the dating game and I decided to put myself on the bench for a while. Three lousy, one night rebounds that resulted in not as much as a call back.

The bench is safe, the bench is easy. The bench lets you get a beer belly from too many nights hanging out at your apartment with Netflix, the bench lets you relax at fairs and conventions and events and helps you get really good at what you do for a living, which is help other people find the happiness you lack. You become talented at spotting how to get someone to join your booth, your company, because you're able to lie to them about what love feels like in the now, even though it's been so long since you've had someone want to get your attention by spinning around and asking if they've got something on their back. I don't know if I'm ready, but maybe I will be when I see Holly's face light up in front of mine and we both say hello for the first time. There's only one way to find out, and as I close the apartment door behind me, make sure it's locked, and walk towards my car, I wonder if this will be the last time I'm ever single again.

A lifetime without LifeTime Clarence said to me, and I told him I was going to use the line the next event we shared together. It was simple, good, and got the point across. The religious dating world should be so easy, but that's what made it so rewarding when you met your wife. Made the wait worth the struggle, worth the risk, worth the swim upstream, the other fish still searching but you finally happy and content to stop, your partner at your side now and the world not so confusing any longer because you have her.

Because you finally find Holly Ryder waiting outside of a four-star sushi restaurant on a crummy looking forest green public bench, tapping her foot nervously until she sees you walk up, hair parted to one side and forehead already somehow sweaty, and seeing this she lets out a small, satisfying smile, stands up, and tugs at her dress slightly to make sure she's ready. And me?

Everything will be alright because I'm ready, just like her. Open the door and hear the satisfying thunk behind me as the door closes on my past life, a new one beginning with more rolls and less sashimi.

REFLECTIONS OF US

"Welcome to Red's, what can I help with you today?"

"Yeah, uh, yeah, yeah, let me think, let me see."

"Sir, we've got sixteen more cars behind you."

"And there was sixteen in front of me when I pulled up. Just let me, now, what would say the difference between the number 4 and the number 7 is?"

"Besides the obvious, sir?"

"Yeah, I, uh, I can't really see much besides that."

"Sir, we've got sixteen more-"

"Yeah, yeah, I heard, sixteen more cars. I'll take the number eleven."

"Sir, the screen is dark. That means it'll be an hour wait."

"Cool, yeah, uh, I can wait an hour for number eleven."

"That'll be fifty seven fifty at the first window."

Car pulls around, nearly hits the side of the building. I slide the window open, fidgeting with the hinges. I'm the money and box tonight. Corporate wants us to switch it up every night to keep it interesting, keep us going, but sometimes it's easier to do both.

Greasy paper slides my way and I hand back two bucks and fifty cents in change, the customer dangling the change in front of me as a tip. "Ain't no fun since LifeTime closed all the strip joints round here, ya know? Gotta tip somebody for my good time." I nod, pretending to care, and point my finger to the second window. "Move forward, sir, we've got cars waiting." He flips me off and the junker shrugs forward to Chris, who's got a wait flag ready to put on top of the car.

After high school ended I didn't really have much going on. My mom told me if I wasn't getting into college I needed to find my way into a job. I nodded and told her I would. Not for me, not for her, not for anything but a way to keep away the boredom. That's how I found Red's.

During my interview the manager of the joint, Mr. David, looked me up and down as if I was one of the items on the menu. "Women don't typically apply to work at one of our franchises as a window operator. You get what we do here, right?" Head, bobbed up and down, up and down. "Well, we'd definitely be pushing the envelope. The customers though, they're going to love your face. And your fucking voice, your motherfucking voice! My God, I'd make you work the box each night if I could. Pay is twelve an hour, no benefits for three months. You'd start next Monday, sound good Miss…Miss Annabelle Reid?" "Everyone calls me Ann, Mr. David. Don't see why you can't do the same."

The night will end soon but until the day creeps round the corner I'll be waiting at the first window taking greasy money. It ain't so bad if you just drone out the sniffs, the looks, the leering from the customers. They know what they are doing, so why hide when they have to hand over their cash? Dirt ain't going to change just because the weather might differ from one day to the next.

At Red's you have a couple options to place your order. The most popular is the drive-thru, only because then you don't have to get out of your car and be seen by anybody. Our location is on a pretty popular road for the locals, and since the town ain't anything like New York or Las Vegas if you get seen here folks are going to hear about it. The drive-thru during the day is packed, during the night is packed, hell, all the time it's packed. We provide something these folks can't get just anywhere.

You can walk in as well, and though I don't work the front counter that often, considering Mr. David wants my face or my voice through the thru, there's chances and low days, holidays primarily, when I get to work the front counter. Mr. David keeps Red's open on the holidays, thinking customers might get an itch around family. Mr. David didn't become manager for nothing.

"Hey, Ann, how we looking right now?"

"Got three more, then it looks done."

"Rush will be down tomorrow, Mr. David said. On account of it being Easter and all. After the three he said we can hit it, he'll count."

"Fine by me, I'm sick of this shit."

"I hear ya on that Ann. But if we didn't do it someone else would."

My mom, she said since I didn't have anything going on I had to get a job. A real one, not some silly desk one. A job that brought me cash quick without having any more to do with school. I'm tired of it, but the cash does come in fast. Real fast. Some of the customers, they keep on hittin' at me, asking if I'm going to be on the board any night now. I shake my head, tell 'em what they owe, then point 'em to the window. If I'm working the window, they want my voice. Say through the box, "Damn, where you at up here?" Or, "You extra sweetheart? Can I get that tongue for free?" Don't know if it's all worth it, staying at Red's. Mom said I needed the cash, we needed the cash, but I don't think I got it in me to do this forever.

Close down the window fast, before anyone else gets the jumps to hit us up. It's a known fact, known through our town at least, that the only joint not worth jumping is Red's. No need to, since we got what you want, whether you know it or not. Close the window and lock it because of the habit, because of the past. I didn't get to manager for no reason now, you know.

Ann and Chris leave their headsets out again and I'll put them on bathroom duty. Third night this week they just drop and run, acting as if they own the joint. They're nice kids, reliable for the last six months or so since I had to hire new. People don't like to be associated with Red's, soils their image. I get it, I really do, but cash is always going to be dirty, that's what they don't get through heads 'til I show them. But if they leave their headsets lying around after clocking out one more night both of them will have bathroom duty. People don't realize that Red's even has toilets, not that anyone uses them. The kids will be up in arms with that detail but it might keep their heads in their work and not leaving headsets out in the open.

Most folks 'round here don't get how much work we put in for our business but fact is, we do. It's not easy competing with a national phenomenon like LifeTime but we get by as businesses like ours do in these times. Thank God what we do is, for the most part, legal. Red's foundation was created because of a need, after all, and not all needs are within the boundaries.

When LT reared its ugly head those few years ago, people forgot what they were upon hearing the news they could find their SoulMate, or whatever shit they called it. So lovey-dovey it makes me sick to my stomach, abandoning all for the love of another. You've got cash, you've got booze, you've got drugs, who needs love? And most important of all, if you really need that pound-and-ground pleasure pop then you got prostitution, right? Wrong, because prostitution is still illegal, stupid fucking country. But that's where Red's comes in.

Red's came out of a need, not a desire. Men, women, they might be all about that love and SoulMate bullshit when they aren't going zonkers for a lay. Sex will do that for you, give you the focus to fix what's wrong with your life. LT was the after, the calm that you wake up to. But the sex, the animal urge, that was being wasted. You can love someone but still want to fuck everything else that walks by you on the street, and Red's knew that. Or more importantly Red's Incorporated knew that.

You know what's easy? Fast food. After a long day at work, what can you make you feel easy? Fast food. What can make dinner a snap, not having to worry about the hour long process of cutting up fucking carrots and tossing them into a piece of shit salad? Fast food. What type of food, when you dive right into it, can just taste so good you want to stop and take it all in like a sunset on an empty beach?

For me it's a cheeseburger with fries, the cheese sticking to the plastic because it didn't take thirty minutes to build in a fancy-schmancy kitchen and didn't cost me sixteen bucks out of my wallet. The burger probably sat underneath a heat lamp, the fries probably left out to dry for a couple of hours, but you know what? It took three minutes to get from under those heat lamps and into my mouth, three minutes flat. Fast food will always be better, because we're all animals on the hunt, on the prowl, and do I want to wait an hour or two for some shit prey to lay itself in front of me? I didn't fucking think so.

Red's took that fast food mindset, mixed it with a little legal working girl action, and created a chain of rent-a-fuck stores. And the whole world exploded for about…five minutes. The religions, my God did they have a field day. Sin, sin, sin, every other word was either sin or Hell coming from their mouths. Folks gave dirty looks, still do I suppose, but you know what? The talk stopped after those five minutes. And you know why? Because people are fucking animals, and we provide their next fucking for around fifty bucks, plus tax of course.

You've got all sorts and types on the board each night. Every Red's operates under the same conditions. The customer can pay for fifteen, thirty, or sixty minutes with one off the board. Two or more is double the rate, though a lot of our customers just take the single. We've got six security guards hired full time, big ol' nasty sons of bitches that'll knock you up proper if you mess with any off the board. They drag you in, all bruised and battered, and throw up against the wall to wait for one or two cops to show up. Red's is a business, after all.

The girls are kept up healthy as best as we can. Full medical, weekly check-ups, the whole nine yards. Fucking jealous half the time at all the perks they get, until I remember why they get them. Not that it's a bad thing, nothing like that. Just not something I'd like to take part in. The girls are on salary from Red's incorporated as well, which means all the cash that flows into the shop under the table, so to speak, is for the shop. The security, the girls, they're all under the corporation. So is the shop too, I guess, but we're all hourly at this point. And hourly is sweet, sweet cash.

Ann and Chris, they'll figure out the drill eventually, and it's nice to have young faces serving old tired ones. Our regulars, the nice ones anyways, they'll nod at the pair of them like old friends. Your best friend in life couldn't match the people not going 'round the community telling folks you're screwing our number three. We keep them busy and they keep us in business, simple fucking science. Now, if I could just get those dipshits to put their headsets away for the evening, I'd be one complete manager. But they'll get it, or they'll be gone. Everyone needs a lay, everyone needs a job.

Ann and I take the same bus home after work each night, but she gets off at 6th and 15th while I get off farther from the city at the intersection of James and Wren. She's really good looking for working where we do, and I sometimes tense up on the bus at night when we stop and another ghost climbs the steps and looks in our general direction. They always glance twice at Ann, and each time their last look is at me, our eyes throwing imaginary blows back and forth. I always wonder if she feels my body sit upright, my muscles filled with the adrenaline rush of possible protection needed. We always sit the same on the ride home each night, her against the window and me on the aisle. She always offers the aisle because of my long legs, but I like to think it's because that way she can stare at me in the reflection.

Red's is a good job because it's helping me save up enough money to leave the state and go away to a nice, four-year college eventually. Or maybe just buy a decent car to look good in. A car that can make its way near 6th and 15th each late afternoon and pick up Ann for our shifts. She'll like the interior, maybe leather or something durable, like pleather. She'll notice my eyes much more closely when she's staring at them from inside a nice new Challenger, or maybe a Mustang, because when I turn towards her at a red light and mention how I just picked it up, she won't want to stare at me through a bus window reflection.

The walk from my bus stop to my parent's house is only two blocks, which made it reasonable for my mom to allow for me to have the job I'm doing. I haven't told her exactly what I do, just that I work fast food at night and don't feel like talking after I'm done. Mr. David makes us keep everything in house, very hush hush, and it's not like I have an official outfit I have to wear to serve the customers. I wear a nice button up, sometimes a flannel, and tell my parents that I never bring home my uniform because the restaurant has a cleaning service do the dirty work. It shuts them up and I can go back to what I'm doing, which is usually nothing.

I walk up to my front door, try really hard to unlock it quietly but never really do. An older house creaks and moans and when I try to get my keys out of the lock they stick so I have to jingle and jangle them noisily until they finally let go. No lights went on in my parent's bedroom so I assume I'm in the clear. I close the door, sigh, and walk down the hallway to my room, flicking the light on the wall and closing my bedroom door in one motion.

It's hard to be alone, even at nineteen. My dad says I'm not alone, that I have family, friends, and now even co-workers. I'm as far from alone as I can be at this point in my life he laughs, slapping me lightly on the back as if swatting a fake moth from my shoulder. I smile and nod, the silent push away that every parent needs and wants. The "your job is done for the moment, please leave me now" look that every responsible adult craves, since it means adulthood is over and playtime, whatever it may be, can begin. For my parents playtime usually consists of Jeopardy at seven, some kind of CBS show at eight, and the news at nine while lying in bed underneath the covers, playing a game to see who can fall asleep first. Loser has to turn off the light and television, kiss the other on the forehead, and laugh at how silly life can be.

For my customers, playtime is getting to have something different, something new, something wild and crazy and still possibly illegal wrap itself around them for fifteen, thirty, or sixty minutes. The it isn't on accident, mind you. To the customers they are objects, but that's the point, right? Mr. David may be crude and disgusting, but he knows what Red's does and why it'll always be successful.

These are women who won't run to these customers families and spoil everything they've worked so hard to achieve. A marriage, a partnership. Stability, safety, the whole American dream. Even LifeTime can't guarantee such a promise.

Before I fall asleep each night I think about Ann. I think about how a girl like her could get swept up in a place like Red's. I think about how her straight, black hair is getting longer and longer each day, and that eventually it might reach the bottom of her lower back, if she lets it get that far. I think about how LT and Red's are two separate entities but one reality, and how Ann could fall further into either one. I worry each and every night on the job that someone will show up at our front counter asking for her, waving one of those stupid pictures and a ripped apart yellow envelope, smiling like an idiot. I'll see it and my heart will sink into the soles of my shoes, crushed by an algorithm from another corporation that only makes sense if you have faith in it. Or maybe you carry the faith because seeing is believing.

Worse yet I see Ann getting offered cash she can't refuse by one of Red's customers one night. See the hand reach up from the BMW, or maybe it'll be a Rolls. The wad of cash, her eyes lit up like fireworks. She'll smile, reach out and ask if they want change. When they tell her to keep it she'll laugh, glance at me and wink, then put her headset next to the till and tell Mr. David she's making her cut for the week in one night. He'll probably laugh and see dollar signs spring up before his fat, piece of shit face. And what will I do?

I'll continue counting down the minutes from Red's to 6th and 15th each late night, and do the same in the late afternoon from James and Wren to the same 6th and 15th, the shadows under my eyes a little less and the flash in my smile, in my voice a little more. I'll wonder if she'll notice the way my face brightens when she says hello, or asks what I've been up to lately. I'll wonder if she'll notice how my muscles tense when I'm showing her what I can be for her, what I can mean. I'll wonder and dream and smile but never actually talk, because I don't want her to say no, or worse yet, that she already sent in for her SoulMate, and she's just now waiting on the results.

I shouldn't feel hindered at this age in my life. I shouldn't feel hindered or hurried or so very much lost. I look to my parents and see the kind of life LifeTime advertises. I see what they are and I wonder if it's even possible in a world where Red's and LT exist. Would it be wrong to just go up to Ann and say how pretty she is? How each night we work together all I can think about is the bus ride home with her by my side? I want to believe in finding a place in this world like my parents have, but sometimes it's too difficult to see through the haze. One day I'll be ready, but until then I'll have our bus rides, our small talk, and our little moments that fill the nights at Red's.

And when I eventually get that new car, be it Challenger, Mustang, or something possibly a little more reasonable, maybe we'll drive away together, our world surrounded by pleather and reflections of us.

ALONE WITH THE STARS

For only an hour?

It's what the bottle says. Think it might be for longer?

There's a bottle, you say?

There's always a bottle, that's how the stuff comes to you. How did you not know there was a bottle?

I always assumed it came in neat, tidy little packages, the kind your parents send when you're away at school.

I never went to school, so how would I be able to understand the comparison? You've got to think before you open your mouth if we're going to get anywhere with these.

If I did anymore thinking I'm afraid your brain might up and disappear on you over night.

What does that even mean?

Means you should've thought about other ways they might've been available besides a fucking bottle.

Doesn't matter now. Show me your palm, all it takes is one.

Just one?

What the bottle says, or do you want me to throw them in a sweet, stupid little package from your mom and dad? Maybe put a bow on top so when you turn you'll think you've got your parent's approval?

I don't need theirs, yours, or anyone's for the next hour.

Open your hand then, got it?

Ready when you are.

Count of three then I suppose. You want me to?

Jesus, you act like we're about to commit suicide. It's just for a fucking hour for fuck sakes. You do the counting, I'm just the brains here.

Talk like that and see where it gets you.

Gets me out of here, on with it already.

Here we go.

One…

Two…

Three.

Some say the cops don't have the tech yet to match up with what we're working with, and the best way to test anything out is to try and run it illegally. That's where we come in, or more where I come in and where Jason merely attempts to keep ahead of what we are doing. He thinks he's so smart, but he's dived so far into his textbooks his fat fucking face might've gotten stuck between the pages. I don't tell him that to his face, but he should probably see in my eyes I ain't so light with his treatment as I used to be. He's nothing but a pile of putty anyhow, but that's why he's needed. Keeps the game going, makes sure we ain't lost by the finish line. I grab my duffel next to me, unzip and rummage through until I pull out my pistol, my lighter, my glasses, and a small can of lighter fluid placing it on the ground next to the back of the toilet. New wardrobe rests inside the bag, silk shirt folded awkwardly. Will a crumpled shirt make me stand out? Dunno, but it's too late as it is.

Right about now we're hoping to break through and take down an armored piece sitting outside the Starbucks across the street from the public bathroom we're occupying, door locked tight. The pill hasn't taken shape quite yet but it will in only a few moments. Lucky we can't be seen, or I'd be worried I'd lose any sort of rep I've made.

Sports bras? The hell are the sports bras for?

Like I said, we don't want to look out of place.

But fucking bras? What if they don't fit, fuck am I talking about, why do we need them at all? We've got jackets for fuck sakes!

We're blending in you bastard, we're blending the fuck in. Don't be stupid this late, not here.

You're thinking way too much into this, and here I thought you had nothing left in that skull of yours. Shirts and pants, that makes sense, hell the shoes even. But bras? You out of your fucking mind?

I'm not going to tell you again, you best watch what spills out of those lips in front of me. Now, repeat what I told you before.

You ought to fucking talk, you know I can walk away at any time you half-wit.

Just tell me again what I told you, that's all I want.

Fucking pulling me down is what you're doing, you know that? Whatever, right, tell you what you told me. We've got one in the seat, the other is dropping off and coming back in four, five minutes at this point. So, unless I'm mistaken, these fuckers better turn on really quickly or we've got another day wasted.

They'll work, they have to.

Nothing is certain until it occurs. You wouldn't know that though, you're just a cog, right? A fucking cog, just like Mr. Goodson said.

Shut your mouth, Jason, shut your dirty mou-

    The change happens suddenly, as if your lips fall off your face and you can't function. Fall to the ground, roll tight against the door but not so much for a BANG, or you might make someone notice, someone walk in and see what they aren't intended to see. The clothes swim over my body, size too large and becoming an unusual covering of sorts.

Jason is writhing around and trying to conceal the surprise mixed with the twinge of pain that roughs up your person once the pill takes effect. Little squeaks here and there, his shoes scuffling along the dirt of the bathroom floor. Almost over now, almost over. Hold your breath, maybe you won't come back up this time, maybe you'll stay one way forever. Pain, just a hint, just a minor amount and then…relief.

Breathing easy, you're body different, your shape not a sad sack but an upright goddess. Stand up as quick as you can, easy now, wobbling is normal, not used to the difference. Lean against the side of the stall, thank God for separate stalls. Take a few more breaths, put on the sports bra, slip on the dress shirt, one size down, the pants the same. Sit down on the toilet in your stall and put the flats on without socks, you don't have time for socks. Inhale deep now, and hope to all that is holy you're hair isn't the same when you open the stall door and head to the sinks and mirrors at the far end of the restroom. Twist the faucets, let the water run across your smaller palms, your smaller fingers, feel the cold mixed with the heat and try to breathe before lifting your head up and staring into a face you don't recognize as your own.

Well, well, well, look at you, gorgeous.

We've got a handful of minutes.

Can't get over your voice, so delicate! You sound intelligent, or maybe that's your tits talking.

To think you've got an education, you slimy prick.

No pricks here you hard-headed bastard.

Funny, but we've got to move. Are you ready?

This baby look ready to you? Let's go grab the cash.

You didn't bring any shit with you, right? I told you, nothing you can't leave behind.

All I got is already in the trash like you said. The separate clothes in the car for later on.

Glad you listened.

Jason holds up the gun, old six-shooter that looks odd in his hand. Look odd in his normal hand, but under the circumstances I'd say it looks even more different. I can't get over Jason as a woman, let alone a woman holding a firearm.

I walk back to my stall and grab the gun, lighter fluid, glasses, and lighter off the ground, throw the rest of my clothes in the duffel and take it over to the trash can near the door. It's difficult to keep on saying good-bye over and over to my life and taking on a new one, but this is what I signed up for with LT. A LifeTime of new lives Rick Goodson said to me, slight smile on his face, hand outstretched for mine. An agreement I could've walked away from, just like I can do now.

I slide the glasses on my face, make sure they are on and ready to record. Toss the bag into the can along with Jason's already disposed outfit and pour lighter fluid all over the contents before flicking the lighter until a small flame bursts to life. I don't have to drop it with the clothes, don't have to do anything but leave. Jason unlocks the bathroom door, peers out and makes sure no one is coming before walking out. I wait ten seconds, toss the lighter into the trash and open the door, stepping out and closing it shut before taking another breath and heading towards the armored truck, gun loose in my hand and steps heavy.

I used to be a regular person, mind you. Not nine-to-five or anything of those sorts, nothing too regular, but I would consider my past self a normal man with a normal life. I rented a one bedroom above a grocery I worked at as a member of the meat department, occasionally moving to the floor if they needed a hand here or there.

Job was a job, life was a life, and if I wasn't working I either ran around the block a couple of times to stay fit or went to the bar and drank on my own for a short while. My weekends were Tuesday and Wednesday each week, which meant Monday night it was me and me alone roaming the streets in the early hours of the morning, piss-drunk and looking up in the sky, yelling at whatever stars I could find in the night.

Regular people can't stay regular forever. I realized how nice it would be to have someone else roam with me under the stars on those nights, yell at 'em like I do, and as lonely as I was I never thought it would be so difficult to find someone to do so. Rejection shapes a regular person, turns them into a puddle of frazzled nerves and broken daydreaming, staring at the pounds of meat behind the display glass and wishing to not be so regular.

On and on and on it went, failed nights turning into early grey mornings, the man in the one-bedroom's bathroom mirror my only real friend. I started picturing others in the mirror after a while, wondering what I could become if I had chosen the other path. Thought of myself as a cop, as an accountant. As a college educated man running his own company. Even as a woman, thinking how nice it would be to not have to initiate, to not be the one holding the doors open for another failed life opportunity. Would I be any lonelier if I was a woman? Different body doesn't mean I wouldn't have the same mind, right?

The profile page for LT was simple enough, just filled out the basics and answered their questions before sending in my $39.99 and laughing at having to incur a charge on my credit card to find happiness. Felt cheap at first, having to pay for love. Made me think I should just hit up a Red's every other night, though that would be more expensive, right? No connection besides sex, I didn't want that kind of life. Wanted the kind where I could wake up each morning and not be in a foul mood right off, feel the warmth of another human being next to me. Know what it was like to be cared about more than just for the way I helped a shopper get a slab of meat into their car and on their way. LifeTime promised me that type of life, that type of world.

When their number first popped up on my phone I believed it a joke pulled on me by another in the meat department, perhaps one of the new folks I hadn't had the chance to encounter quite yet. I didn't answer then, and I didn't pick up the second ring-round. Wasn't until the third buzz-buzz-buzz in my pocket to finally reach in and slide to answer. The voice on the other end was polite, female, young sounding. I cleared my throat after my short hello, thinking this might be it. I was young-ish, she was young, right? No one unless they are someone in your life would call me in the middle of my day, right?

Her name was Heather and she said she worked for LT's headquarters in the city. She told me her superiors were fascinated by my profile and wanted to inquire about whether or not I would be open to coming for a visit. She said they would provide a free lunch and just wanted to spend an hour or so discussing possibilities for my SoulMate, as I was truly a unique case. Me, I thought, the unique case. The regular guy, somehow taking a leap into the sky and joining all the stars.

The front of the building was all glass, real fancy, the door handles shaped into a capital L and T. I didn't know which one made sense to grab so I took hold of the T and hoped it made sense. These people thought of me as unique, which meant I had to make choices different from others, no?

The receptionist at front had my name already in the book when I walked in, or probably my picture considering they knew who I was at this point. Gave me a nice little bottle of water with the LifeTime logo on it, drank half right then and there when she told me Ms. Knoll would be out in just a moment. Nervous, body uncomfortable, as if I wanted to leap out of my skin and observe the meeting from a safe distance. The ping of an elevator off to the right announced Ms. Knoll's arrival before the clacking of her heels did. Professional looking, young as her voice made her out to be, maybe twenty-six, twenty-seven at the most. A young business professional, and here I am standing in my old jeans and Vans as if I know better, as if I belong. Silly, but this is what they wanted, right? Her hand is soft, handshake strong. This will be the beginning.

She tells me she works directly under Rick Goodson, the head for LT's R & D, and he's currently in the conference center to begin our meeting. She hands me a pamphlet menu that lists ten or so food items and says to pick as many as I like. The words lobster and mignon stand out immediately as if written in block and bold and I feel a little overwhelmed. I'm not use to this. I work and live in the same block, rarely if ever leaving the confines of the safety net I've created.

Leonard, at last we meet face to face! Come in, please, come in.

Leonard, this is Rick Goodson.

Heather, stop, you embarrass me. Leonard, don't feel pressured to call me anything but Rick, no Mr. Goodson here. We're here to discuss you after all, so I hope you feel comfortable after a while. Would you like anything to drink? We've got it all.

Nothing for me, thanks.

Not anything at all, you sure?

Yes, I'm, ah, I'm sure.

Well then, I will stick with what I've got and we can sit down and get to the business at hand. Heather, thank you for bringing Leonard to me, I'll call you when we are ready for lunch. Leonard, keep the menu, you'll need it after our meeting.

The door closes behind us and Rick motions for me to take a seat at the conference table next to where he is at the head of the room. Shaded glass sits across from me, the lobby downstairs in view from his office. The air is warmer in here than the entrance, ripe with his cologne and some other sweet smells I can't quite figure out. He sits down in the chair and smiles at me with shiny pearls between pale red lips.

Well Leonard, I wasn't so sure we would ever see you in house here, to be honest. Not our style for the most part, as you are aware from putting your profile together. However, after reading your profile our team here sent it straight to me, and after I looked it over I've got to say I am very pleased you decided to come here today.

I appreciate the kind words, thank you sir.

Ah, Leonard, you're forgetting our first rule. Please, call me by my first name.

Right, thank you Rick.

Wonderful, glad we're on a first name basis finally. Leonard, I want to be as straight with you as I can here, and the only way I can do so is to be as honest as possible, okay? See, I picture big things in our future Leonard, and I mean ours and not just mine or yours. Ours, as in the two of us working together to do something simply extraordinary. Reading over your profile, I see unmolded clay Leonard, the possibilities endless, just as they should be for your life as well as LifeTime's.

Here at LifeTime we are building, shaping our future along with the countless others in this nation, and I want you to be with us when we grow even bigger, moving past the normal and expanding into a realm, a world of our own. Leonard, I did not simply ask to meet with you today because of your unique profile, I had you come here because I want to offer you an opportunity unlike any other you have been presented with, and I know this because I know you, Leonard.

I have to say…Rick, I'm floored, but what do you see me doing? My profile was just about myself and my work, what do I fit here?

I like how you asked that, Leonard. "What do I fit here?", as if you already belong. Your honesty is refreshing, and we need more of that honesty here, that's for certain. However, you fit here at LifeTime because of who you are, what you do, and what you said in your profile. You are a normal person, an Average Joe, and one who can blend in easily. I need someone who can blend, do you understand? I need you, Leonard, because you are alone. You are alone with nothing in the world besides your job and the skin on your back, and yet you blend in so well no can see how lonely you are. You are the butcher, the neighbor, the barfly, no?

Isn't everyone alone who looks here? Isn't that the point?

Good question, very good question. For the most part yes, we do get many lonely individuals. That doesn't mean they aren't married or in a relationship though, if that's what you are asking Leonard. We have all types send us their money because we are always alone, are we not? What we do here is actually find the person you are intended to be with, instead of being with a falsity. But your loneliness, your personal loneliness, is astounding. You have never been the center of attention, have you Leonard? I would expect not, seeing and knowing who you are. This is what makes you unique, the ability to blend, to be recognizable and at the same time, nothing. I need that.

But why? Why do you need me if I'm nothing?

Leonard, I do not mean offense, no, no, no, not at all! Being nothing is what landed you here! Running through our data on you, we had nothing! You are a ghost, you are a breaker, a glitch. I envy you, Leonard, I truly do, because you can be anything and anyone you want to be, and that is why you are here with me today. There will be others that we hope to be like you, but I know with certainty no one will match you. You are clay, and I can help mold you into whatever you want to be.

How then? What are you wanting me to do?

I'm glad you asked. When I set out to work for this company, I meant my time here to be more than just as a name and a body. I wanted to be revolutionary, and I believe we are on the right track. However, a great company does not stop when it has reached the top of the mountain, it builds on that mountain and becomes greater. Our R&D wing here has been working with some of the top labs in D.C. to build material capable of changing the genetic make-up of human beings. Tests have been running for over a year-and-a-half, and now we feel we have developed a sustainable method, a practical, safe means to become someone else.

Become someone else? Change?

Change everything, for an hour, only an hour. At least that's what the tests have yielded. One hour to be an entirely different individual, can you imagine? For couples it adds a spice. A way to pretend, to dream. For others? It lets you be reckless, mysterious, a millionaire, heck, a billionaire if you have the cash. But more importantly, this changes how you look, whether it's the color of your hair to what type of nose or mouth you have, or even what your sex is.

You're telling me you've put something together to make me become a woman if I wanted to?

Leonard, how would you feel about leaving your old self for a while and becoming something extraordinary? You have the opportunity, all you have to do is take it. A LifeTime of lives, all lived within one.

How do I go about changing then? Sounds painful.

Well, there is of course a slight bit of pain involved with anything revolutionary, but we're hoping with your help we can figure out a way to, well, iron out the kinks. However, the way you would go about this is by swallowing a small pill, maybe half-an-inch long at most I'd say.

A pill? Like Asprin?

Precisely, which you might need a lot of at first, coincidentally. A pill for anything you want to be. Want to see how you would look with a six-pack and no tan lines? We've got a pill for that. It's dyed orange actually, you'll see it. Want to be as tall as a center in the NBA, or short as a little person? We've got pills. All of it would be available for you, all at your disposal. The only things I would need from you are to not ask why, and your loyalty. You'll be well paid, your apartment covered, hell, we'll get you a car if you need one.

Why a car? I thought I was just testing the pills, I can get here just fine on bus.

As much as I would like to keep this in house, I want to see about expanding into the public, and what I mean by that is having you, Leonard, go out and test what people think of the end results of these pills.
For an hour at a time I want you to run through the D.C. area like a rat let loose out of the maze. We will deliver a package to you each week with pills and, of course, your assignments. I will expect you to record the experiments. On the first delivery there will be a separate package containing glasses with a video camera built in. Black adjustable frames, quality camera. After each experiment you will upload the videos through your computer and store them on a flash drive, which you will deliver here at the end of each week.

What if something happens? Goes wrong?

You destroy the glasses and, if you can, all the evidence before you can't. Pretty simple, right? Your body language says you're interested. I trust this has at least not been the most boring meeting you've ever decided to attend, no? How about this, let's have lunch, talk about life and nothing work related, and then come back around and see how we feel. What do you say, Leonard, does that sound all well and good?

　　Regular becomes different, different becomes extraordinary. My mirror became a glimpse into another world that first week after the packages arrived. There was a letter inside with the pills, explaining each day of the week what I would be doing. Monday I was to take the pills with a green label and have a conversation with one of the regulars at the bar in the evening. Tuesday during the day I would take the pills with the pink label and do the same with a diner down the road, but then that evening go back to the bar as myself and see if the same regular I had spoken with previously recognized me at all from the night before.

　　This was the routine, the rhythm, and for the first two months I would continuously do the same exact thing, making up personas and having sideways conversations for thirty to forty minutes at a time. I didn't mind the work, only because it wasn't work. It was talking, and I was not only able to get paid handsomely for it, I was able to keep my job at the grocery as well. Then Jason arrived and everything changed.

He told me he worked for LT and I thought he was the delivery man I'd been missing every Sunday afternoon. When he didn't leave and instead walked up and handed me a letter telling me to open it and read, I got the feeling I wasn't going to like what was written on the inside. New assignment, new partner, same pills for me but not for him. Working together meant those new assignments would be out of the ordinary. On Monday and Tuesday we had to get pulled over for speeding with me as a pill persona and then with our normal selves, he driving luckily. On Wednesday and Thursday I had to get caught shoplifting in a pill persona with Jason waiting in the parking lot behind the wheel of a running car and then return the next day asking whether or not they caught the perp yet as my normal self. If I didn't make it to Thursday I would smash the glasses and pray for mercy.

The assignments began to take on a new meaning with Jason at my side, and the urge to back out of all I'd gotten into increased every time he knocked on my door. Illegal became a word to me, just another way for Rick to test out his new product. It was clear why we were doing what we were doing, to show the strength of the pills and know we were really different one day to the next. I couldn't help but stop sometimes in the evening and stare up at the sky, wishing I was back to being regular and yelling drunkenly at the stars I should've just left on their own.

Today was different, I could tell by the look in Jason's eyes when he handed over the package. Felt heavier than normal, even for a Monday, and when I ripped it open two pistols fell out onto the kitchen counter, along with two separate bottles of pills, both blue. Jason was standing at the door waiting as usual, not wanting to come in. The assignment, just one, written in bold. An address, a description of the pills, and a statement. ARMORED VEHICLE, RETURN THE NEXT DAY TO THE SCENE OF THE CRIME

AND ASK FOR DESCRIPTIONS FROM THE WITNESSES. I took a deep breath, let it out slow. This one was going to be different.

Put the gun away, Jason.

We didn't test these fuckers out, what if they don't work?

Do we really want to be using 'em?

What if we have to, you didn't think about that now, did you?

Just focus on what we're doing. Just focus on what we're for.

Attempted robbery, I don't know how I feel about this one.

If it fails we won't fall. Just run

And dodge bullets.

Right, and dodge bullets.

Our voices, changed, the glasses no doubt picking up the feed. I've already been a woman twice so far, but this time is different. I've never had to run in this persona, and now if things go poorly I'll have to try. Walking is difficult enough, figuring out the balance, the movement. We're at a slow pace from the bathroom, and I keep on wanting to turn around to check if someone has decided to go in after we left but it's early so I doubt it. I can't look bad, looking back means wasted time, and we've only got one chance at this.

Do the guns work? What a question, a good one actually. Jason is sensible, even though he's a loud mouth. But is anyone that sensible if they agreed to go through what we're currently moving towards? To just pop some pills and decide to go on and take down a truck full of cash?
We're standing parallel from the truck, the driver not noticing us. His partner, probably three minutes away at this point. It's going to have to be quick or nothing at all. I look over at Jason and he's adjusting his top, pulling it down lower to reveal more cleavage. He notices me

watching and gives a wink before walking towards the truck.

He knocks on the window, which is probably the right way to go about it. The driver looks down at Jason, gives him the "move along" finger wag. Jason knocks again, smiling at the driver. He sighs, opens the door, and looks down at Jason. "Ma'am, I'm going to have to ask you to step away from the vehicle or-"

He doesn't get the last word out, the gun pulled out from the back of my pants and aimed at his chest. I put a finger to my lips and motion for him to move to the back of the truck. "You're insane, you know we don't hold that much, don't you? This isn't going to end well, why don't you just walk away and I'll pretend I just had to stretch my legs, make something up." I shake my head and Jason lets out a short giggle. Is he having fun, or is it just the nerves?

The walk to the back of the truck feels like an eternity even though it lasts for a few seconds. I force the driver up against the side of the truck, looking to see if any pedestrians or other drivers have noticed. We're in front of a Starbucks in the early morning, there's bound to be people showing up sooner rather than later. I want to say this is it, we don't have to actually rob the truck, right? Just get the game rolling, get an audience, then leave.

I point for Jason to pat down the driver, make sure he's clean. He takes the gun from his holster and pats down the rest of his body, coming up with nothing. "You could've just walked away, you know that, right? You can't be this stupid, it's going to be over in a matter of seconds. You aren't going to get away." The driver acts like we're dead, but I don't think we are. Not if we walk away, not if we leave right—

Jason doesn't see it but I do. The driver was right, we aren't going to get out of this. His partner, gun drawn and aimed at the back of Jason's neck. Jason notices I'm not moving and his face drops, realizing what waits behind him.

Drop the gun ma'am, don't do anything you'll regret.

Leonard, drop the fucking gun.

Place it down gently, easy, and no one will get hurt. Do you understand ma'am?

Leonard it's over. Just fucking do it already!

Ma'am please calm down, we don't need to get worked up over this.

I'm not getting worked up, I've got a fucking gun at the back of my head and I don't want to fucking die because shit for brains—

Ma'am, settle down.

Just put the gun on the ground you asshole.

Listen, we've got the police on their way, all you have to do is drop the gun and you won't get hurt.

Ah fuck, what am I going to do? Why am I here, why did I go along with this stupid fucking thing?

Ma'am, move away from the truck, place the gun on the ground, and kick it over to my partner. Do you understand?

No, I don't understand. I don't understand how I was foolish enough to roll with a plan concocted for the sake of a memory game I now realize I shouldn't have been a part of. I want to lower the gun, but I can't. I should've just stayed the regular guy but I didn't, and now all I want to do is go back and be able to stare up at the stars and act the fool. The only thing I do understand at this point in my life is that I should've just stayed alone in my loneliness, and not tried to bring anyone else into my world.
I can't go to jail, that's a fate worse than death. In less than forty-five minutes my body will revert back to its original state, and then the guards will have more than a batch of confusion on their hands. I can't let that happen. If anything is going to be said about me it will be after I can no longer hear it. And that's my only option at this point. There's only one path to being the regular guy again, leaping

off of this perch and falling from the stars into the ground waiting for me below.

I slowly move the glasses off my face before dropping them on the ground. The guard behind Jason has his gun now trained on me, and from Jason's face I can tell he knows what I'm about to do, devastation an interesting mask upon his mask. The guard says something but I can't hear it, blood rushing through my ears and adrenaline high.

All I have to do is take a step, smash the glasses, and my life will be over. The guard will pull the trigger of the gun he has on me, and I'll die on the street as a woman, and then thirty minutes later a man. I just need to take one, hard step and remove the evidence. I look over at Jason and flash a grin. Wonder if his book smarts helped him figure this one out? I inhale deeply, my eyes wide open and ready.

Here we go.

One…

Two…

Three.

LIFE ON PAWS

"Why do we keep pets in our homes, in our lives, in our world? For companionship, for fun, for the joy of coming home after a long day at work and seeing their happy, little faces bouncing up and down at us, we their entire universe for that one, perfect moment. Shouldn't the same be said for your relationship with another human, and not just your favorite animal? We here at LT think so, and that's why we are very happy to welcome all of you to our first ever Pups for Proposals festival!"

What am I doing here, with a rent-a-dog of all things? It's not totally a rent-a-dog situation, Buckley and I have met on previous occasions, but I don't know what kind of food he likes or the walk & waddle he'll do when he needs to take a shit on the ground. God forbid he does take one, won't that be embarrassing. A dog owner gagging on the fumes of her supposed dog's product when she tries to pick it up and toss it away. I'd probably be kicked out, wouldn't I?

Buckley belongs to my brother and his family, but they are out on vacation for two weeks exploring the country all packed up in a mini-van he bought six months ago. Do I really want that, a van packed full of people who love me? What if one night I'm driving with my lot in the back and start drifting off, wake up too late and crash into an eighteen-wheeler head-on? Mini-vans are too much responsibility, I don't know how he does it. Good thing they left Buckley behind, because a dog full of loved ones in a mini-van? Sounds like a nightmare.

My brother tells me Buckley is a mutt, which doesn't help me when I'm trying to fill out the form at the Pups for Proposals festivals entrance. Mutt isn't on the sheet for me to circle under Breed, the panic already settling in nicely before I've even stepped past the chain link barrier and into the festival grounds, let alone try to find the love of my life. What am I doing here?

I'm worried any person I do meet today will automatically leave me once they hear Buckley doesn't belong to me. I can try to explain he's my brother's dog and I'm just a hopeless romantic who wanted to act on a couple of animalistic urges myself, but I feel like that kind of talk might dig a further hole with any love I plan on finding today.

Buckley is sitting next to me, looking around with his tongue hanging out of his mouth, ears perked up whenever he hears a random bark in the festival area. I hand over the clipboard to Volunteer Jane and she smiles and hands over a blank nametag for me to fill out. I could lie about everything with the nametag, fill it out and become someone entirely new. How exciting would that be, to walk in one way and become another in an instant? I could be from overseas somewhere, Europe born and bred. Or maybe lie and say I'm a doctor, a writer even?

My fingers are trembling slightly from the thought, pen vibrating and wanting to write something unique with the black ink in my hand. Eventually I stay original, writing out JORDAN in large, block lettering. I take the nametag and stick it on. Jordan and Buckley, on the prowl at Pups for Proposals. Look out, here we come.

My brother and I couldn't be more different, and I think Buckley can sense the difference when we enter the park aka festival event center. LifeTime rented out a local park just for Pups for Proposals, and I can't imagine how much they had to fork over to install so many tents and booths around. The air smells of fur, food, and fun according to Volunteer Dave at the front entrance, but as I hand him my ticket all I can smell is dog shit and a hint of despair. What am I doing here with Buckley the rent-a-dog at my side? What if Buckley finds love before I do, or worse finds love with a less-attractive female dog? Will he still be happy, even though he knows it's all downhill from here? Will I, considering it'll be my brother's problem and not mine after today?

First glance and I'd say there are more vendors here than potential suitors. I begin wondering if the vendors brought their dogs as well. God, to make a sale and then find a SoulMate? That would be a hell of a thing. Maybe I should pretend to be a dog food rep, no? Buckley stares up at me and gives me a "why aren't we moving" type of look. Right, we need to move on from Volunteer Dave, there are other's waiting.

First step is always the worst part, but with Buckley leading the way I nearly forget the importance. I'm just trying to make sure he doesn't get off his leash by the time we've left the main entrance and head into the park, music loud from the stage off in the distance and the air still pungent with shit left unattended.

Being single for the last year has been a period of growth for me I didn't really anticipate. At first I was a mess, just like I should've been. My brother, with his mini-van full of happiness, he and his wife helped out a lot. I've never really been much of a cook, and for a while my microwave and I were closer than kin.

The stove hated me, or maybe it loved not having to worry about burning away. Living as a microwave, now that was where you wanted to be. Quick heating and you're done, a sprint and nothing more. You aren't mangled, you aren't exhausted because you've got so much power behind your method, the food coming in just to be heated up. The stove now, that's a slow, tired life. You and the microwave both heat up, but you burn like nothing else around you, and you burn, burn, burn until you're crusted and damaged and hate the world around you. And then, as if spiting everything you stand for, your owner sees how ragged you look and decides to use the microwave exclusively. I'd hate me too if I was the stove.

Dating wasn't any easier, since I hadn't done it in quite a long time. My brother's wife put together a few here and there, blind ones where you could find me impatiently waiting at a table for two, nibbling nervously at a breadstick and wondering what would happen if I dipped the stick of bread into the flame from the candle in the middle of the table. Would I be kicked out for creating a torch to try and guide my way out of darkness? Cheesy yeah, but if it impressed my date or made them giggle, wasn't that the point of all this? Haven't done anything of the sort yet, but if I found fire and a breadstick at Pups for Proposals wouldn't that be a good start? Buckley would probably disapprove, eyes looking me over and wondering what in the hell he was doing at an event like this with a sap like me.

Near the entrance a giant board stands upright, a schedule laid out for the festivities. I arrived an hour after the Grand Opening

Celebration because I decided to pace back and forth in the driveway of my brother's home for thirty minutes, coming up with any and all thoughts on whether attending Pups for Proposals was a good idea. I hadn't thought there would be a celebration, but what did I care, right? It has been an hour though, maybe my SoulMate left after the opening. We hadn't talked about it, how would I know he would be on time? We haven't even met yet, let alone established what time we thought would make the most sense to arrive.

Concerts going on all day, but the moment that really caught my eye was the second to last event of the evening. All the schedule said was "A Chase Ball", the times 7:30-9:30 PM. At ten this sucker shut down, at ten all would be over. Pups for Proposals meant you found love through your dog, and this was the final event before the Closing Reception, whatever that meant. A Chase Ball was the real ending, the spectacular finale, and from the line forming at the entrance to get in I knew this is what really mattered. I take a glance at my watch, see it's six and breathe a sigh of relief. The anticipation is building inside my body, and though I've no thought on what A Chase Ball could mean, it can't be bad, right?

Buckley leads and I follow down the dirt path that separates vendors from each other. I get called at a few times, asking what kind of pooch Buckley is, asking if they can pet him. Thank God there aren't any kids here, that would be embarrassing. Why there would be any is a good question, but I would hate to have Buckley swarmed by sticky fingers and idiot grins. I'll have to make sure my SoulMate doesn't want kids, not that I wouldn't adopt any if given the chance. Adopting is what dog lovers like, right? Buckley was adopted, he can back me up if the time comes. He's the one I'm here for, right?

The park's population is growing as the day turns to night, Buckley and I no longer waltzing down the dirt aisles but walking slowly, edging past and under arms and through legs. Buckley seems to be enjoying himself, smelling other dogs and glancing around and smiling his toothy grin every now and then at the world around him. I hope Buckley doesn't think this is a normal Saturday evening, that would be depressing. Hell, it's depressing realizing he's probably never been to an event similar to this one before, different dogs all around him. The smells, I can't imagine what his nose is picking up, the air around him full of new parts of a life he never knew existed. Overwhelming for a dog to leave all he's known and venture into a brand new way of life, even if it is for only a moment. Terrifying but exhilarating, an entire world of possibilities out there for the taking.

I'm questioning my outfit at this point, worried A Chase Ball requires a more upscale wardrobe than a flannel and shorts with sandals look. Pups for Proposals is held outside, my attire is meant for outside, and looking around at my fellow patrons of this first-time event I would say I'm in the right. However, I just can't help but thinking I'm doing something wrong with what I'm wearing. Do I need a hat, perhaps? A fedora to show I'm not just a bum with a dog who was able to cough up the entrance fee.

My brother hates it when I wear a flannel with shorts, only because he thinks it doesn't make much sense. Cold on top but not the bottom? It doesn't make much sense but I feel comfortable wearing the outfit and the first piece of the dating game to remember is that being comfortable promotes confidence, and confidence not only runs on down to Buckley as a sense of respect, but to the men I have the chance to speak with at A Chase Ball. Will I get to speak with one? I've no idea, but I can't let them know that. Men aren't meant to know how worried I am to have the opportunity to speak with them.

I wish I hadn't reverted back to my old way of thinking after I became single again, but it's difficult to learn something new when the original is right there waiting to come home. You can't teach an old dog new tricks, right? That's funny, I can save that for later possibly. Might make someone laugh, though I wouldn't know who yet exactly. We're at Pups for Proposals, dogs are relatable.

There's no wind which is great, just a light breeze coasting in every couple of seconds and hitting my face, pushing my hair back in a playful manner. Most of the vendors have gone home at this point or are packing up their belongings. The outdoor stage is brightly lit ahead of me, tangled lights dangling off the edge and all around a wooden dance floor, put together in front of the stage probably during the Opening Celebration. The dark of the night greets me and I smile, a real, genuine smile. I don't know what about tonight has me riled up, but the feeling is here and it moves through my person like a bolt of energy and hope. I wouldn't know Buckley was still around if the leash didn't pull forward, but he's leading the way right to the wooden dance floor in front of the stage, the swarm of dogs and their owners all gathering near.

I don't know if the polished wood can hold all of us at the same time, but maybe my SoulMate will think the same thing and decide the grass next to the stage is better for whatever we may be doing. More than dancing? I think not, what would be the point of a dance floor? Or is it a dance floor? Do dogs like the way the wood feels against their paws? Buckley might, and maybe my SoulMate's dog won't mind either. Are they really my SoulMate, considering Buckley isn't my dog? I don't know if I could handle finding a partner for my already married brother, since it's his dog. Awkward is a word I can use to describe such a conundrum, but a word I don't think does justice to the situation.

A woman stands on the stage above the dance floor, a backing orchestra behind her. Next to the woman and in front of the orchestra are some of the volunteers, the remainder of who hasn't left yet. They are flashing toothy grins at the crowd as if taking pictures, sometimes waving back at a participant or laughing in their direction. The volunteers are either holding on to or have large cardboard boxes at their feet, and I realize I might get a free item from the event, which would be a good reminder to keep in case I do meet someone. Then again, it could very well be a treat for Buckley and the other dogs.

The orchestra came out to raving applause from the crowd, and though it isn't the biggest one I've seen assembled it's decent size for having to work on an outdoor stage. We're all packed together, sardines standing with their dogs, wanting to know what comes next. The woman raises her arms and the bubbling conversation from the crowd and stage ceases to exist. She smiles, takes a breath, and begins to speak.

"We at LifeTime are just…overjoyed at what a fantastic turnout we've had at our first ever Pups for Proposals festival! Knowing that so many out here were able to attend this special gathering fills our hearts with the love you will know very soon!

"As you are all no doubt aware, each of you were hand selected by our Love Experts at LT to attend tonight, your profile matching up with another individual that could be standing next to you right now! We have helped most of you charter flights, buses, rental cars, and we know because you made it here, because you stand here with us tonight, you truly believe love exists, and love exists for you!

"As I continue speaking, our volunteers will come around and hand you a candle. I only say this now, but please do not let your dogs eat the candle. You will only get one, and I would hate for you miss out on our next festivity. Now, once you have your candle please do not light it. Our volunteers will come around again with lighters and light your candle for you. Our hearts full to the brim, our candles burning with the love that surrounds us. A Chase Ball is your chance, ladies and gentlemen, to find your SoulMate. A chance to stare into the eyes of the one you are meant to be with, and how will you know? Simply because your dog will guide you to them."

I answered a question on the LT profile saying I was a dog person rather than a cat, and I think it's coming back to bite me. I don't know how LifeTime operates, specifically how they find out who a person belongs with, but I do know that questions is what brought me here tonight. Buckley's fuzzy brown tail is illuminated by the light from the candle, the slow wag a signal of trepidation perhaps? Diving right in, now that wouldn't be me. That's not Jordan, sounds more like a doctor from England named Riley, but definitely not Jordan.

The crispness in the air after my candle is lit by Volunteer Rose, the heat from the flame warming the tips of my fingers. Fire all around me, some laughing quietly to themselves, others breathing heavily and anticipating the next part to come. We were all brought here for a purpose, for a form we filled out and a nearly forty dollars we paid. We were all brought here to find the one meant for us according to the company running the event. I look at the candle for answers and get nothing, my mind blank in a rush of adrenaline and terror. Buckley doesn't seem to be moving, do I just stand and wait for Buckley's dog to come over with the owner holding onto the leash behind? Do we take our dogs off the leash? What am I doing here?

The band has started playing, a nice number I don't know but the strings section is at full volume and I get so mesmerized by the lead violinist's bow going back and forth I almost don't notice Buckley's leash gently slipping further and further out of my hand. My thumb hooks at the end of the fabric and I look down to see Buckley moving through the crowd. I shrug my shoulders at no one in particular and realize this must be it. Is there some type of pheromone in the air that he's attracted to? How is Buckley the mutt going to find my SoulMate?

We weave through the crowd, the rest of the owners either looking at the stage or their dog. The night is alive with music, the dance floor dark and the candles looking as if they are suspended in the air. Buckley has got a scent now, his leisurely stroll interrupted here and there by questioning sniffs and snorts followed by grunts of pleasure and the continued pace of an animal hopefully find another dog with a decent to normal looking owner.

I'm not really worried about which of these owners I could end up with as a SoulMate, even though my mind would like someone who not only can stand me emotionally but look fantastic in any and all kinds of outfits. That's the dream though, and after I became single again I threw the dream out.

Breaking up with the love of your life and hoping to find, well, the love of your life again should be easier, and maybe that's what LT is up to with Pups for Proposals, but I don't know if I'm ready. The haze of smoke around the gathering blurs my vision, and instead of looking forward all I can do is stop and pause in the present, take a breath, and try to not break down in the middle of what was intended to be a happy, life-altering moment. The tugging on the leash persists, and as I push away the smoke I look down to find Buckley sprawled out on the grass, lounging peacefully.

He is my brother's dog, so it would make sense he wouldn't find anyone if my brother already has a wife and family. I didn't expect my time on the dance floor to end so suddenly, but Buckley looks like he's done with the event and just wants to call it a night. I'm there with him at this point, but before I can wander towards the exit a chocolate lab comes up to Buckley and begins sniffing cautiously around his body. Buckley's ears are perked and his tail is still, his body now rigid and no longer couch potato quality. He hasn't lifted his head up quite yet but as the other dog continues sniffing I can sense the eventual next move.

Buckley wrenches his body up quickly, standing next to the chocolate lab for a moment before both exchanging more sniff pleasantries, their bodies intertwined for a moment as if two snakes crossing paths in the grass before separating, Buckley's body thrown once more on the grass but rolling around now on his back, swift side-to-side movements as if he's got an itch on his back he can't reach. The chocolate lab is bouncing around Buckley at this point, the leash looking like it's about to snap from the pressure. A man's voice follows, yelling in a playful way. "Take it easy there gal, we've got all night."

He's not terrible looking, kind of pudgy in the middle but it's not terrible, clearly a gym member. Tall, much taller than me, not alarmingly so but still significant. He's got on a dark-colored flannel and what look to be stained navy blue jeans, and I can't see his shoes but I wonder if they are sandals. His glasses give off a reflection of the candle in my hand, and when I lower the candle I can see has a significant amount of facial hair, like a bird's next but hopefully a little more well-kept. I'm flustered by his sudden appearance, and I'm guessing it might just be an accident.

"Sorry about that, let her roam since you know, let the dogs lead the way. My name is Walden, but my friends call me Wally. The dog currently playing with yours is named Bog, and she can kind of be an idiot sometimes."

"No, no, that's okay, no worries. I'm Jordan, and this is Buckley. It's nice to meet you." I run my hands through my hair once, twice, hope he's watching his dog but know he's not.

"Can you believe they put this together without sending out a picture beforehand? I heard from some others we get the results at the end once we try to leave or something."

"Yeah, I, uh, yeah that's a little odd considering what we are all here for. You said we'll know whether we were right at the end?" What is wrong with me, of course he said that. Why am I being stupid, he's right here and I'm acting like Buckley when I need to be me, be like Jordan.

"Yeah at the end supposedly. I don't know if that's really happening but you never know."

"Huh, well that's really interesting."

"Right, that's what I was thinking. Well…"

"So, I, well…"

"I like your hair, neat color."

"You can see it?"

"I actually saw it earlier before we did this candle thing, whatever this means, right? I thought it was different, in a totally good way of course."

"I'm not offended, don't worry. Thanks."

Crickets for a moment, silence all around the four of us. The world holds its breath.

"I actually wondered if it was going to be you, you know?"

"Really? Why?"

"You looked like someone I could get along with. I didn't know what to expect from all this, and the others I just got tired talking with. You seem interesting. Plus we're wearing similar shirts, so I mean, fate, right?"

"Ha, well, thanks again, but I don't know that."

"We've got a while, do you want to sit and talk, or should we, I don't know, let these dorks play some more?"

"I think if we're going to do anything we should see if this is it."

"Really? Already? You sure?"

"Well no, but isn't that the reason we're here?"

"I, uh, I guess you're right. Why waste time?"

    The walk from the stage area to the front entrance, now exit, might be one of the longest moments of my life so far. Walden walks with Bog next to me, Buckley keeping pace, the pair leading and prancing as if show dogs.
At the front entrance now is a long fold-out with two people sitting behind it. There's three lanterns on the table in front of them, and I can see a pile of papers along with a stack of yellow envelopes next to them. My heart is beating hard, the thump-thump-thump filling my ears. I tug at the back of my flannel, smile for no particular reason, and realize deep down I'm leaving after this moment either way.

    I know she's saying something because her lips are moving, but Volunteer Michelle clearly isn't saying anything, right? I look over at Walden and he's giving me a puzzling glance, and all I can do is ask, "Excuse me, could you repeat that?"

"What is your last name?"

"Spaulding, my last name is Spaulding." She smiles and looks down at the papers while the other volunteer leafs through the yellow envelopes until he stops near the bottom.

"Jordan Spaulding?"

"Yes, that's me."

"We'll need to see your identification before we can let you see the contents of the packet."

I reach into the front pocket of my shorts, pull out a packet of tissues, a credit card, and my driver's license all in one go. Walden laughs and asks, "Wait, what else do you have in there?" He acts like he knows me already, but all he knows is what he sees, right? How would he know if we were meant to be together if all we did was meet at a pet event, and me with a dog that is my brother's? Does he know the truth about Buckley, the rent-a-dog?

"Right…this looks great. Enclosed in this envelope will be a picture of your SoulMate, as designed by LifeTime, and will include their documentation including name, home address, email, and phone number. Thank you for using LifeTime for your love-finding services, and have a great rest of your night."

Life is funny, right when you come down to it. Funny that I get a message from LT asking me to come to a Pups for Proposals event when I don't have an actual dog. Funny that I accepted the invite because I want to feel something again, want to be wanted by more than just my brother and his wife to take care of Buckley every now and again. Needed by another person not because I can house sit but because I'm sick and tired of using the microwave, because I'm done with leaving the stove on its own. I don't want to go back and fall into the same routine of meals at six, bed by eight, my pillow stained with the tears of yesterday in the morning. I want something better, something new, something different.

I want the opportunity to fall in love, not just the possibility. It's why I chose LifeTime, because I don't want to waste anymore of my time falling into the same traps, the same games, the same thing over and over and over. The envelope, regardless if it is Walden or not, gives me the chance to actually know my SoulMate. I know the envelope in my hands is a sign of better things to come, and I have proof that I'm meant to be here. It's hard not to smile and see what lies past the candle-lit dance floor, through the limbs and instruments of the orchestra on stage and into a better life ahead, with or without a rent-a-dog at my side.

ANONYMOUS LOVE SONGS

You just came back from…wait, no, that's not right. Reign it in, pause for a moment. You returned, sounds better. You returned the other night, purse slung over your shoulder and your dress looser than when you left. You didn't have to open your mouth to tell me where you'd been, your body told me all I had to know. It's over, Jane, and I don't want this to go to court, but if you try to take anything it will.

Dan, that makes more sense, right

"He wanted that last part in there? For real?"

You know how clients are, for what they pay we can't remove it.

"Speaking of, you see the show we just put out?"

They make television shows now? I'm so out of the picture here.

"Yeah, pretty crazy shit, right? Like they don't get enough money."

I'll check it out after I'm done with this, what's the name?

"Love Songs, corny as all hell. I'll let you get to it. Remember, drinks tonight, everyone is coming. You better show up, it's been six times, SIX times I've asked you."

I've got a lot of work, I don't know if it's the smart thing to do.

"Ryan, Ryan, Ryan, work will always be there. Nights out with people you work with, now I don't know how often that kind of magic springs up."

So far every Friday for the last six weeks or so.

"Maybe you're right, but then again, maybe you won't be."

I'll…probably go. Just let me finish what I'm working on.

"As your editor I'll be severely disappointed if you don't! Call me at five and tell me you're coming with us, Ry."

I'm generally surprised my face hasn't developed a weird, out of sorts set of tan-lines from my computer screen, considering how close I have to get during the evening to read the letters on my keyboard. I have lights in my office but I try to conserve the energy, convinced the electric bill shouldn't raise above forty dollars a month. It's not my fault my parents installed in me a logical thought process for how to carry a frugal lifestyle. Heck, it's only me out here anyways.

I've been working for LifeTime the last two-and-a-half years as the Head Postman for the Lettering Department, a fun little title to make sure I won't have any exciting future job opportunities if I think about leaving. How do I even put such a job description on a resume and actually expect to get employment?

Essentially what I'm paid to do is write specific letters from new LifeTime clients who haven't had the decency to tell their partners they are leaving them for another. Or, such as the letter I was discussing with Dan, my main editor in Lettering, those that have extra initiative to leave their partners high and dry. It's really not too difficult of a job considering most of the material is provided to me, but there are those fun moments where I have to be creative.

Stunning, slightly, how many letters I have to churn out a week. Some days I'm looking at two or three passing my desk, a standstill where Dan won't stop coming into my office. Then there are nights like tonight, when I've churned out fifty previously and, when everyone else is gone, still have more and more to push before the post goes out on Monday. For everything LT says about how successful their relationships are, it's quite difficult to be on the front end of it all. To see lives beginning right before my very eyes, my words part of those new beginnings, those new paths, it makes me feel uneasy inside. As if all the negativity will eventually catch up and overwhelm me.

Dan gets upset with me because I've only gone out for a beer with our department once in my time with LT. I would probably be that way as well if I were Dan. He likes to make people happy, strange for an editor of letters and mailings intended to do the exact opposite, and when his longest tenured co-worker isn't feeling the love he makes a face or leaves you a voicemail expressing how upset he is. I like Dan as my editor, like him as a boss, but I'm not really sure about him as a friend. We're colleagues, and just as it is with everyone else in our department I want to keep it that way. When you get too close to someone they are bound to hurt you one way or another.

Leading a single life in a place surrounding you with love has turned into a fun challenge for me. I didn't expect to be alone at this point in my life, didn't plan all my steps carefully. I've gone on a few dates here and there the past few years, dates that usually ended at the restaurant. Maybe it's my demeanor, or the words I use in conversation. Words like "disappointed" or "separate checks". I don't mind going at it on my own anymore, not since I'm always seeing what love creates each day at my desk. Shopping for groceries is not only fun, since I'm the one deciding what to get, but cheaper as well.

Some would say I lead a very boring life, and I would have to agree with them. My mom likes to tell people I take the conservative approach lifestyle, my dad nodding and saying I only like to save my words for when I absolutely have to. I'm not quiet, just observant, a man meant for a life kept in the darkness rather than the spotlight. That is, of course, until tonight. Tonight, unfortunately, will take my conservative approach lifestyle and throw it out the window.

Tonight is the night when I decide, against better judgement, to have a drink with Dan and the office, and somehow find my way a week later where I sit now, backstage at the new LifeTime show Love Songs, about to go in front of what I'm told is a national television audience of over twenty million viewers expecting me, quiet and simple me, to sing for my SoulMate.

"I'm honestly, Ryan, I'm not shitting you, I can't believe my eyes right now. Are you, is he here, guys? Hold up, let me, just one second."

Dan's pretending to rub his eyes behind his beer, and they're loving it. I don't get a reputation for nothing, and as Young Pete, Andrew, Allison, and Laurie laugh at Dan, I smile and see how quickly I can drink my water to make the excuse to get another.

"You wouldn't believe it, but this is the closest we've gotten to have the entire department here at one of these things. We're missing the, ah, we're missing the new gal, but hey, at least we have Ry. Andrew, what's her name again?"

Andrew shrugs and I do the same, even though Dan has told me. I don't get out of my office space much, but I do know of her only because Dan rushed in and said I should start dating her immediately on the first day she was in our office.

"Ry, she's cute, you'll like her. She's just like you, quiet, all that stuff you like, and she's got a nose piercing. You ever been with a gal with a nose ring before? Seems exotic, right?"

We share one similar personality trait and you think I'll like her? And I don't know if it's really good protocol to be talking like that about an employee.

"Oh shut up, you know what I mean, and get out of here with that nonsense. You need to just meet her, that's all. You'll see what I talking about. She's been asking about you, wants to know you. Just meet her tomorrow or something."

We're at a local pizza joint that does cheap pitchers on Friday, and Dan tells me for the fifth time how he had to make sure to reserve the table on Wednesday and not Thursday, just in case.

"You don't drink, Ryan? Really?"

I just, I don't know, it really just doesn't interest me.

Young Pete jumps in. "Ryan, you've got to tell me how you do it?"

How I do what, Pete?

"How you relax without booze after writing the letters all day. What's your secret, man?"

Young Pete is only three months in but likes to come into my office every day and have me check wording on a sequence of letters he'll send out the following Monday. I like him, but I can already tell by the way he comes into work at 8:20 instead of 8:00 that he isn't planning on sticking around for much longer. Not an easy job writing paragraphs of words filled with venom day in and day out. It's no wonder he's turned to alcohol so easily, not many people grow up seeing how expensive it is in restaurants and at the grocery store. Though to give Dan some credit, pitchers of it for five a pop is by far the cheapest I've seen in the D.C. area. Pretty much giving it away at that rate.

"Ry, don't listen to Petey, he's just happy you're here."

"Ryan, I did not, I would not mean offense. That is not what I meant, I swear."

The rest of them are at the other end of the table, talking about something I can't hear but I wish I was a part of at this moment. I don't like dealing with a drunk, even if it is Young Pete, and Dan knows this about me. We have worked for over two years together in the same department.

"Ryan, here's what I'm thinking. You have one glass, on me, and if you want you never have to come to one of these nights again."

That's silly, you know I came out tonight because I wanted to.

"Ry, Ry, just give me one…God…damn…beer. Just one, and I will shut up for the rest of our lives together. Forever, I swear."

But I like our talks. You're my editor, I don't know how productive our working relationship would be if you didn't talk.

"You know exactly what I mean. Ryan, come on, peer pressure. We ain't getting any younger, just one and you'll have me off your back."

He used ain't which worries me for a reason he'll probably roll his eyes at. Young Pete has moved on and jumped into the other conversation, rubbing his finger over a slice of pepperoni pizza from top to bottom before picking at one of the pepperonis and throwing it back into his open mouth. It's just me and Dan, and Dan's got this glint in his eye, the same glint he gets when I try to turn a one-page letter into a three-and-a-half page masterpiece. He won't be backing down, and I wonder if we'll be here all night in a strange sort of stalemate. I give him a cold stare and he gives me the largest grin he can muster.

Get me a glass and I'm in. But you're pouring.

In college I was the same as I am now, frugal to the last cent. My parents were already paying so much for my education and without a meal plan at the cafeteria, to save money of course, I had to get by with as much as I could on the little I had. With that frugality mindset as my main source it was far easier in the moment to get the cheapest beer for a get together, put it in the fridge and then see if there was something better in the house already. Don't get me wrong, I like alcohol as much as the next person, but what Young Pete didn't understand was the job doesn't wear on you as much if you have plenty in the bank account. I could grab a flight to anywhere at any moment if I needed too with the money I've put away. I could start over whenever I needed to.

When Dan poured the beer into my glass and I brought it to my lips, I could tell it was the cheap beer I usually bought. Five dollars might have been too much for a pitcher, but with not only Dan but the entire table watching I couldn't just put it down for the sake of quality. A free glass of beer is a free glass of beer.

One free glass of beer turned to two, then three, and then suddenly I felt good enough to buy the next pitcher, yelling out

FUCK IT, much to the delight of Dan and the entire Lettering department. The pizza joint was extremely crowded, and as I stood with Dan in line to get another two pitchers, my vision slightly impaired but I was doing fine, I was going to make it, I overheard why it was so crowded. I turned to Dan and yelled, LOVE SONGS IS ON IN FIVE, YOU HEAR THAT? EVERYONE IS SO EXCITED FOR LOVE SONGS, DAN!

He never looked so embarrassed and happy in one moment since we've worked together, and I couldn't stop laughing. In the back of my mind I feared our work relationship was in jeopardy, a friendship on the horizon. I couldn't see how I'd afford one of these nights every week, but at the time I didn't care. All I wanted was beer, pizza, and Love Songs by LifeTime.

Saturday's sun poked through the blinds of my one bedroom apartment's living room window, and I realized in a groggy state I had fallen asleep on my carpet and not the couch. Luckily I didn't wear my glasses. I'm convinced they would've been victims from my bender with Lettering, crushed under the weight of my drunk skull. I roll over and let out a good morning belch, the mixture of pizza and beer on my breath disgusting. I try to piece together what happened, slowly, but my phone won't stop buzzing in my pocket. Someone is calling me way too early in the morning.

I reach into my pants and pull out my phone, swiping and expecting to see maybe three missed calls. Instead I'm faced with thirty, my eyes nearly jumping out of their sockets. Thirty, and it's only 9:30 AM? On top of that there's sixteen emails, and I wonder if I'm going to make it through the day. I decide to check the emails first, only because I don't necessarily have to respond to those if I don't want to. I'm guessing those are safer as well, probably just offers from some of the mailing lists I've subscribed to about weekly or monthly deals. When I see the first email in my inbox, I realize just how wrong I can be when I'm hungover.

Dan, what exactly happened last night?

"Oh my God, am I the first person you called? Please tell me you already got a response. Please, please, please."

Dan, what did you do?

"Ry, listen, I did nothing. You can't get mad at me for this, it was all you, man."

You didn't help, I don't know, push the button or something?

"If me and Young Pete could've we would've, but you were on your game last night. I couldn't believe it. Calling in to Love Songs is one thing, and you're crazy for that, but there's no way they accepted you, right?"

Dan's voice, drowned out as I read the email over and over again. The words, bouncing around my head, oh my head hurts so badly. "Congratulations", followed by "profile", then "contestant". I can't concentrate, I can't believe it.

Dan, did I sign up to be on Love Songs? He laughs on the other end, and I can see his stupid grin in my head.

"You bet your sweet ass you did. And more than that, you're a celebrity now, Ry."

Out of the thirty voicemails from my parents, concerned family members, former friends, and my co-workers, the one that I listen to the most over the next ten minutes of my life is from Young Pete. He had sobered up at this point in the night but I had clearly continued on, and though it's slightly muffled you can hear me rather clearly in the background. As I'm listening to me finding fame, I search the show on Wikipedia.

Love Songs is one of those American Idol-type shows, but instead of competing you match. There are three judges, and they bring on twenty contestants each week from around the nation and from those contestants they try and create as many relationships as possible, so ten if it's a good night.

The way you discover your love is through singing karaoke with another person, in my case another woman, on a song of your choice. The show goes man, woman, man, woman for the order until everyone has had a chance to sing their songs. The audience votes on which "couples" sounded best together on each song, and from there a relationship is born, if the percentage is high enough.

The final piece of the show that throws everyone for a loop though is the Instant Connection meter, and this is decided by the three judges. An Instant Connection is earned if all three judges really feel the chemistry between couples during the song is so palpable, so electric that the song has to be stopped and the pair must be together. Basically, if you're last and everyone gets an Instant Connection before you, you're fucked. Unless of course a fan calls in and somehow fights an Instant Connection on live television from a local pizza joint.

"Ryan, I don't know if what you did has ever happened before. Honestly, I don't think they field calls that late."

Dan and I have taken our out-of-work friendship to another level it seems. He came over immediately after I hung up and took me to breakfast, saying it would help. He clearly hasn't showered yet, a funk coming off his person and his hair sticking out sideways. He can't stop smiling.

What do you mean it's never happened before?

"Okay, I know you don't watch it, but the phone call stuff is great usually because they do it in the middle of the show. Like during the breaks, when they are changing the songs or something. Typically it's just wacked out chicks or big fans of the show saying how much they love a couple or how great one of the judges are, you know, stupid shit like that. Sometimes, very rarely, they'll bring people on for an Instant Connection, and most of the time it's people wigging out or crying because they're stupid and happy."

What LT is looking for.

"Exactly Ry, exactly. But you…oh, what you did was simply…triumphant. One of a fucking kind."

How I got through is still a mystery to me, but I can ask the producers after the show, now that I'm here. All I do need to know is I've already signed three shirts from the audience on my way backstage, and I'm kind of worried it won't stop there. I'm not sure how I feel about becoming an icon from a drunk speech, but then again, as Dan said, I was one of a fucking kind.

"Folks, folks, folks, I'm being told we've got a call on Sam and Molly's Instant Connection, and according to Rhonda this call can just not wait. Folks, we're going to take the call, because it's from someone who works for LifeTime, and if you don't know already, we don't get this opportunity that often! Everyone, calm down, calm down, let's be quiet for a moment. Rhonda, I'm ready, send it in…we good?

"AHEM, this is Ward Warren and you've reached the number one show for finding your SoulMate, Love Songs! I want to warn you that you are in fact live in front of an audience of over TWENTY MILLION HERE AND WATCHING AT HOME! Now, we know you work for our beloved LT, and we are truly honored to have you on. So, what's your thoughts on Sam and Molly, and more importantly one of the quickest Instant Connections in show history?"

Holy SHIT, did you just say twenty…twenty million people? Oh man, I'm not ready for that.

"I, uh…we are live here, pal, and we here at Love Songs don't really appreciate the language."

God, I'm sorry, I'm so sorry…DAN, DAN SHUT UP, I'M ON THE PHONE. War, War you wouldn't believe it, Dan made me do it. He said if I had one beer then I wouldn't have to come out with the guys again. He said, War, and now I don't know what to believe. War, get this: five buck pitchers. Tell all your friends you got there tonight, five bucks at Buca's, five bucks.

"Ha, well, right, well, right, clearly my friends and I didn't ah…we didn't expect this. What's your name, pal, and more importantly, what do you think of Sam and Molly as an Instant Connection?"

War, is that, is that your real name? You ever hear that song, the one where war…where war is looked down on. My name, Ryan Riggins, my name isn't in a song like that. Makes you wonder what it's good for. But Molly and Sam, War, my goodness. Love, War, love is real! Not for me, but for Molly and Sam, talk about SoulMates. If those two don't last, none of us will. Unreal, War, UNREAL! And I thought it was all fake before-

They cut me off after that, and according to the voicemail from Young Pete I was none too pleased. However, the worst part would come later, and in a way I did not imagine it happening, at least not for a frugal, conservative approach man who had never thought about being on a television show.

Dan, I can't sing.

"That's not what you told them last night. The buzz around you is crazy. Ward Warren couldn't get enough of you after the show, you should've seen the news after. You made the top of the hour."

I'm going to lose my job over this, aren't I? I'm going to be fired, this is it.

"Nah, no way. They're so excited it's just, it's all just so crazy! You've got the entire company behind you, everyone wanting you to find love in front of America. It's going to be amazing, just wait."

Dan, I just told you, I can't sing, and I'm going on a show in front of everyone to, you guessed it, sing. What in the hell am I going to do?

What I tried to do was block out all the phone calls, the emails, the knocks at my apartment door every hour I was inside. Agents, managers, people wanting a piece of the pie, and if it wasn't them it was my coworkers or my family. My mom was ecstatic because she pictured grandkids, even though she didn't just come right out and say it. My dad asked the questions I kept asking myself: was it even worth it at this point? The week flew by, my work left on my desk, letters not written. And then on Sunday afternoon a town car pulled up in front of my apartment.

"Okay Ryan, now you know this will be live, so let's try and not throw out the language from the other night, sound good?

I, I want to apologize for that, I was…I was under the weather.

"HA, I love this guy! Under the weather! Bud, you're fine, just ease it back for Ward, will ya? And more importantly, have fun out there. You won't get this chance again to find a SoulMate."

But this is…that's not the point, to find a SoulMate out on a stage in front of so many eyes.

"Ay, man, it's not. It's better than having to find out from a photograph though, isn't it?"

LifeTime thinks Love Songs might last forever. I just need to last an hour and try not to have a breakdown. I don't get to meet any of the women I'll be looking to spend the rest of my life with before the show, but I do get to meet the men who will go on stage before me. Not surprising I'm going last, and all I can think of are wave upon wave of Instant Connection. That's a good thing though, right? I don't need a partner, I've got my parents and my apartment. And then maybe one day a small dog or a large cat, whatever I'm in the mood for. Who's got time for relationships anyways, right?

"What song do you want?"

Doesn't the girl, doesn't she pick that out?

"Not if you're last pal, you get the pick. What'll it be?"

I don't know, you pick.

"Me pick? Really?"

Well, I mean, I trust you.

"You don't even know me."

I don't know anyone here, except for Ward, and he probably hates me.

"He hates everybody. My name's Joe. You're Ryan the Loveless, right?"

The Loveless, really? How do I have a nickname already?

"God, you should've seen Ward after the show. Amazing. Wish they had you call in every night. I'll pick a good one out for you, something different. Good different."

Thanks, I appreciate it. You wouldn't happen to know when we go on, would you?

"Start in an hour, but you'll be up near the end. They do a delay so I'm guessing hour and-a-half or so from now since it's two hours. Think positive, you'll be fine!"

Most of the contestants, or so I'm told, like to sit in the waiting area before they go on. Let's them have a moment to relax before trying to win the heart of another in front of so many people. I'm going last, and to see everyone go out before me and possibly not come back, well, I'm already nervous as it is. Plus, if there are any Instant Connections I'd like to see them sooner rather than later.

My nerves are tingling and I'm not even up yet, but there is just something about the show powering up, the cameras everywhere, the laughter, chatter all over the building. Love Songs is about to begin, and as I stare backstage at the first contestants, Jim from Portland, Oregon and Mary from Miami, Florida, I feel like passing out. And…we're off.

Ward is excited, beyond actually. I can hear it in his voice over the speaker in the waiting room, where I've decided I'd be more comfortable considering what's happening on the stage right now. The waiting room itself is nice, bottles of water and cans of soda on a fold-out table, chips and dip next to them. Couple of couches here and there, and three large mirrors near the doorway. I could just sneak out the door, climb up the stairs and bolt the opposite direction of the stage, a stain on Love Songs only by name. Would be easier than what's going to happen instead. I've got a while before my turn.

Eight Instant Connections, eight in a row. Ward is losing it, the other two judges, I don't know their names, are speechless. Never occurred in the history of the show, and from the hollers and yells it looks like there's going to be a ninth. I've turned my phone off earlier, and though the temptation to check it is strong I hold off because I don't want to hear about how great the first nine couples were. I can hear them just fine, and I think they might have hired professionals just for tonight, just because they knew I'd be on.

I keep on telling myself they can't make me a fool since I feel like one already, but then I drift back to the professional "let's fuck up Ryan Riggins for life" angle again, which makes me wonder what they are paying them. Is there a going rate for ruining a guy's life on national television? I feel like I deserve a cut, considering I was the first to try when I called in drunk.

The soda they do have they probably overpaid for, or maybe they got the bulk rate from somewhere. Maybe a tie-in with a sponsorship I bet, LT isn't stupid. I'm trying anything to not think about what's coming in less than thirty minutes. I'm not an open person as it is, my time spent doing things I'm comfortable with. Work Monday through Friday, sometimes a Saturday or Sunday here and there if I need to play catch up. Dinner or lunch with my parents, if they guilt me into it, and then a two or three mile jog around the neighborhood every other to make sure I don't fall out of shape. Maybe some online shopping here and there, and of course going to the grocery store on Sunday and hanging out with everyone else preparing for the week to come. I don't make time to be crazy, to be outrageous. It's just not who I am.

"Mr. Riggins, you've got twenty minutes until we hit commercial and bring you up. You need anything else before you go on?"

I, uh, no…no, I'm good. Twenty minutes?

"Nineteen now, we'll come and get you. Remember, it's supposed to be fun! Big smiles!"

Right, I'll be ready in nineteen. See you soon.

Go back to the nearest couch and flop down. Rub my hands over my face, let out a long winded sigh and trying to piece something together besides hopelessness and fear. Fear at being rejected on national television, fear at going up and people hearing my awful voice. Dan, he likes to please people, he's the one that wants to make everyone happy. I can't just be like him on a moment's notice. I take my time, I listen. I should've asked them for a six-pack of cheap beer, anything to get me where I was the other night. Any kind of help would work.

A knock at the door, three minutes later. These people never quit apparently with the preparation, but maybe it's Joe with an update on my song or perhaps they heard my thoughts and brought down a bottle of whiskey or vodka to dull the nerves. I open the waiting area door and instead of finding a person with a headset and an agenda I open wide to a woman standing in the doorway, arms folded loosely, jacket held off her shoulders and the glint of a nose piercing catching my eye. She looks familiar.

"Mind if I come in?" The first thing that comes to my head is she's a Love Songs groupie, which I immediately shoot down as a terrible thought. I get out of her way and she walks towards a couch and sits down while I close the door. Where do I know her? Television? This show the other night?

I thought they didn't allow us to meet before we go out there.

"That's what they had in the contract or whatever we signed earlier, but since I didn't have anything better to do in the next fifteen minutes I thought I'd go for a walk. Autumn, nice to meet you. "

Well, I, uh…well. I'm Ryan.

She's pretty but not gorgeous, which makes me feel better for some reason. I'm not Mr. Handsome of course, just a normal looking LifeTime employee who couldn't keep his drunk mouth shut, but I felt with a gorgeous person singing next to me I would shrink in the spotlight.

"You aren't drunk all the time, right? The other night isn't normal or something, is it?"

I don't usually drink too much, if at all. Beer at restaurants is typically double or triple the price than at the market, so to answer your question, no. Last week has taken me very far out of my normal. Is that why you came over here?

"Yeah, I mean that was part of it. The other was to meet you before we go on. I can't believe they make you wait in separate rooms."

I think it's a love at first sight angle. LT loves playing up immediate love to the audience. Makes the product pop.

"First sight is what you think? Kind of funny. You seem like you're freaking out. It's got to be weird going on a show funded by the company you work for."

Especially if you didn't know about the show until last week.

"What? Really? How is that even possible, Love Songs has been on for over three, four months already?"

The department I work in is a specialized one. We send letters out, so it's not like we're a major part of LifeTime.

"Every part helps it go, though, right?"

I…yeah, I guess so.

She's looking at me now, waiting for me to ask what she does probably, but I feel like we've run into each other at one time or another and I just need a moment to figure where. Or she probably sees what she's going to have sing with and is already planning an exit strategy. I don't go out on many dates for a reason.

If I had to put a price on my conversational skills people would think there was a going-out-of-business special, or maybe a Black Friday type of deal. I try to be polite but I just don't get it right, and yet she's smiling next to me, not leaving to go back to her waiting area. Maybe I should relax more, considering what we're about go and do on stage in a couple of minutes. Maybe all of this is a wonderful mistake.

So, uh, you go on dating shows often? She smiles, a real smile, the edges of her mouth crinkling a bit. Or maybe it's more of a smirk, I can't tell.

"Only when I'm not busy at work. You?"

Not typically, but the offer to humiliate myself in front of twenty million viewers seemed too good to pass up.

"We've got five minutes, we can still leave and get a coffee or something. No one would notice, they're all working on a television show."

Buying coffee in public is a loss financially, just so expensive. But, if we didn't have to be on this show and I wasn't going to be fired by LT if I left suddenly, well…I guess what I'm saying is that'd be nice.

"You don't really leave your bubble, do you?"

I'm told I take the conservative approach in life by my mom.

"Well, you're here now, which means you might not be as boring as you think. By the way, I have to ask, but what song did you pick out? Because they told me you'd already picked one out, and I was cool with whatever."

A knock on the door, followed by another headset and a disapproving glare at Autumn. We both smile, kids caught with our hands in the cookie jar. "Time to go you two, let's move. The judges are ready."

I've only been on a stage once in my life, during a first grade Thanksgiving theatre spectacular. I played one of the pilgrims, and I'll be damned if I didn't give the best performance out of the entire group. I spun the lines perfectly, showed the right emotion when the Native Americans sat down at the table with us for the first time, or when I had to kill the turkey. I was on, at least in my own mind. I think that was the last time I've had so much confidence in what I was doing, and it was in first grade.

It's a commercial break, but when Autumn and I walk out onto the stage and are shown where we will be standing and where the screens with the words for the song are, the audience lights up, whistles and hollering heard in-between claps and chatter. Ward and the judges are smiling at us, and when I look up for a moment he catches my eye and gives me a wink. I didn't think this would be a pleasant experience, considering what we are doing, but I didn't think it would terrifying. Why are my palms so sweaty? Is my forehead doing the same?

She smells nice, which calms me down some as Love Songs comes out of commercial and Ward starts talking with the audience about us, the next pair of singers "looking for that special someone". They already told us Autumn would go on first and then I would follow. I hoped to not trip, even though it might be funny. She said I was funny, would that be slapstick or dumbass? I'm thinking too much, but wouldn't anyone do the same?

Ward is wrapping up, the woman across the way behind the curtain has her hand raised, and I know with the drop Autumn will walk onto the stage. She can probably hear her name anyways, but that's how things are done here apparently. I've got to talk to her, even if it's right before. I tap her shoulder and she turns around.

Hey, uh, I, I don't know if this means anything but I just wanted to say thanks for doing this with me. Definitely a smirk this time, but even in the faded light behind the curtain I can see her blush slightly, which throws my stomach into a fit of warm knots.

"We'll be fine out there together."

The lights, so damn hot. I'm trying to keep a smile on my face but I'm terrified. I don't really know where to look but I know I'm standing in the right spot from where they told me earlier. I see the judges and try to block out the first few rows of faces, my heart beating so fast I'm worried I'm going to have a heart attack. I steal a quick glance over at her and she looks calm. I don't really know anything about her save for her rule-breaking, and I'm supposed to somehow pull off an Instant Connection with her? I'm pretty sure all they did was hire actors, which would explain where I saw her from. Probably a commercial, or an ad online. Ward begins his dialogue, my ears fuzzy.

"Ladies and gentlemen, we have made it to the final pair of the night! Tonight has just been spectacular as we have had a record breaking nine Instant Connection couples! What a glorious night for love!"

The applause is shattering, the faces in the crowd smiling, laughing at me, at her? Or is it all just happiness at seeing people find each other? Is this what the other departments of LT feel like all the time?

"Now, I hope our audience is ready for these two, because as you all probably know, we've got two LT celebrities on stage with us tonight for our final song!" Did he just say two? "Of course, you've got my main man on the left, the one and only Ryan Riggins, who left us speechless with his phone call last week. Ryan, bud, how does it feel to finally have a chance to find that special someone?" He's staring at me, they're all staring at me. Oh god, what have I gotten myself into.

It, ah, feels okay.

The audience laughs, Ward smiling. One of the other judges chimes in, the woman with the tall hair. "Just okay, Ry guy? You're here on national television, about to possibly sing with the woman you'll spend the rest of your life with, and it's just okay?" I swallow, hard, and realize that pleasing everyone is really difficult. Makes me appreciate Dan a little bit more for trying so much, the bastard.

I'm just, you know, nervous. I want to make sure it all goes okay.

The crowd awws and I'm off the hook. I haven't even sung yet and already I'm feeling the spotlight. Ward starts up again.

"Isn't that special folks, what a guy. Ryan, we hope it goes well for you tonight as well, we really do." I'm nodding like a woodpecker at a tree, for no reason other than to get the attention away from me. "But Ryan, as you know, it takes two to tango. And as you are probably aware, that's why we have Autumn Evans on the stage with you. Let's give her a round of applause."

It's hard not to smile up here, and as the claps rain down I realize what it means to be a star for a second. These people love me for being drunkenly honest over a phone call. As Dan would say, it's just crazy.

"Now, as you know, here on Love Songs we don't like for our contestants to know each other before they get on stage and sing their hearts out. However, what we have on stage right now is something special, and I will tell you, I've been excited all evening for this one. I mentioned we have two LT celebrities on stage tonight, and I wasn't lying. We have two LifeTime employees with us for our final song of the evening, and get this everyone, they both work in the same department! Finding love, and only a few feet away! Ryan, Autumn, we're all ready to hear you sing, so without further ado let's get to it! Tonight, for our final song, we've got a special one handpicked for this moment! The words will spring up on the screen ahead of you, and of course will play at the bottom of the screen for our audience at home to sing along too!"

I'll hear about what I looked like later in the three voicemails from Young Pete, Andrew, and Dan after I've left the stage and finally turned on my phone again, but right now I don't have that luxury. As the audience cheers I turn towards Autumn, my mouth slightly open. I had seen her before in passing. I'd heard about her from Dan, from Young Pete. The new girl in the Lettering department turns her head to me and smiles, nodding to the stand. I feel for the microphone stand in front of me, fumbling for a moment before the music starts.

I led a boring life before last week. A life spent behind a closed office door Monday through Friday, sometimes on Saturday and Sunday, consumed by the material I thought was important. A life I thought was important from how much money I saved, or how little risk I took. A life I felt comfortable with, felt safe in, and now see was nothing but empty. A life waiting for the living to actually begin, and all it took was one five dollar pitcher and a co-worker I hadn't truly met yet to finally help me find the life I'd been missing...all in front of a national audience.

I turn towards her and raise my eyebrows before giving an exasperated smile. She laughs and reaches out and grabs my hand in hers, palms sweaty. The music starts, the words pop on screen, and we drift away with the lyrics.

JUST IN MY HEAD

I ask him if he ever misses the ocean and he just laughs and says Florida is only a drive away. A drive to where the water is clear enough you can reach down and remember what it was like to be a baby in a bathtub, swim out to the middle and float on waves until you're gone and away. I sigh and smile, shaking my head. A man-child in a giant bathtub, splashing his way to the middle of nowhere.

His name is Jack but I call him Greg because it's his middle name and he likes how there's a G on both sides of it. He's been at LT for less than a year but more than six months, I can't remember. I can't remember much before he came here, at least nothing significant. The days all blend together when you're going about the same task over and over, especially if it's for others to find happiness. Seeing so many happy couples together only makes you hate the world a little more each day.

I've been at LifeTime for two years working as a Level Five Continuation Coach, East Coast Region. I didn't just start at the fifth, had to see a lot of others crash and burn before me, but I'm glad how far I've come, and where I can go from here.

My job is simple enough. I call, email, or sometimes visit different couples that have used our services, checking in to see how their relationship is and if anything is wrong. LT has built a reputation on finding your SoulMate, and even though the higher ups believe in the algorithm, they still send out people like me or like our recruiters to make sure it sticks.

Of course, it always does work out. People typically hate being wrong regardless of the situation, but if it's about a leap of faith they took on a relationship? There's boldness in this world, and then there is pure stupidity. The lot that gets themselves mixed up in LifeTime wants to believe they are the bold, the daring, not the idiotic, the foolish. They find love in the numbers, and the numbers can only be right, which means if they don't find love through LT's match, it's them who are incorrect, not the company providing them with happiness. Or they just fall off the deep end, commit suicide, you know the picture. I'd like to say it happens only a couple of times, but then I'd be lying.

Greg's first day was an exercise in how to draw unwanted attention. I was going over an email I was sending to a client in Connecticut when he knocked on my office door. I stopped what I was doing, frowning at the closed door. I knew I didn't have a meeting nor a lunch visit with my sister. She was out of town in California, working on a new LT project called Match Me Tonight, a television show idea.

I got up from my desk and tugged at the handle with my right hand, my left curling up into my jacket slightly. A tall man, hair parted to the right in a messy style. He smiled, asked if I was Cheryl? Is this Cheryl Hansen's office? He leaned on the side of the door, fingers gently running along the frame as if he'd always been waiting right outside of it.

Being a Continuation Coach is not as simple as being one of the normal Roadies. You've got to stay on top of the client, letting them know though they are right they must be wrong at the same time. Happiness is our business we say, but in reality sadness drives us. If a client finds his SoulMate off-putting, disgusting or, worse, strange, we tell them the reason is not the SoulMate but the change in scenery. For the most part these people have led one way of life for the entirety of their time walking the planet. It's shocking to find the one you're meant to be with so quickly, and even though it truly might be an error on our part, we never play it that way. They've already spent their money, why waste their time too? They did what they did for a reason, and now they've got to put the work in.

Greg and I are similar in more than a couple of ways but different as well, which made my work life become easier than what it was before. When I tell my family, my friends, the neighbor down the street walking his dog what I do and who I work for, they always picture perfection. Surrounded by love, how grand, how wonderful, their faces contorting into an awkward show of happy that I don't want to stick around for. Greg, though, he lived for those moments. He looks for them, wanted to feed off the positivity these people threw at him. His clients were his friends, his familiar. It only took him coming into my life for me to figure out I was the same.

His office was a floor below mine but I stop in on my way up to talk with him about a television show or movie he'd seen the night before. He'll wander up and knock on my office door and a smile will hit my face from nowhere, my hands typing out nonsense on the screen he won't be able to see when he walks in, my mind telling me to look, to act busy, busy, busy.

We share these moments, these times, and I daydream about who he goes home to each night, wondering if she knows how lucky she has it. It's been nearly a year since we've been together, and though I already know the answer we play the game anyhow. Greg loves LT because it gave him the happiness he craved in the form of a yellow envelope with a watermarked photograph inside, and I suppose I did the same. We're both the same, for the most part, and why would our search of happiness end any differently? Work for what you love, but more work for what you feel thankful for. LT gave us everything, including each other, and now I don't know what to think anymore.

"You got that hun?"

"I can't, I'm putting on my make-up."

"You couldn't do that an hour ago? We're going to be late."

"I wouldn't be late if you had just cleaned up your beer cans from the night before."

"Don't go and blame me for us being late, you know I hate that. My cans were in recycling where they are supposed to be."

"Don't lie, Kyle, you know you're wrong, just admit as much."

Double dates with our SoulMates. Greg brought it up as a way to break the ice his first week on the job, and here we were on our fiftieth outing. Said it would be a good way to get to know each other, since we were the only Continuation Coaches for the East that seemed to talk with each other. I wanted to tell him as a Level Five I had to talk with a Level One for training purposes but when I caught his eyes I couldn't just say no. I wanted to get to know him more. He had this way about him, how he carried himself. He was someone worth knowing.

LifeTime doesn't make mistakes. We're a company that demands results, positive results, and if for some reason a SoulMate pairing crashes and burns we blame it on the client, not our system. Which is why I know I'm being foolish tonight to think any differently about trading what I have for something unsure and impractical. What I have is Kyle, and what Greg has is Jessica. What we don't have is each other.

Kyle isn't an alcoholic but he likes liquor. I'm convinced I was made for him as a way for both of us to get over our indifferences with this life. I'm bitter, possibly mean to some. Greg says I'm misunderstood with a smirk on his face, letting out a quick laugh when my face scrunches up in annoyance. I'm not bitter, I just can't hand stupidity. Kyle gets that about me, I guess. He's always telling me he does at least.

Jessica is bubbly and fresh and so in love with Greg it makes me sick. I can't stand going out with them together, her rubbing the back of his neck and then laughing loudly at every little word that escapes his mouth. First it's Chinese, then Italian, then American, Kyle ordering Greg beers once, twice, three time until they switch seats and I'm stuck with Jessica again, her hand rubbing his neck while we talk about which celebrity is screwing the other behind his wife's back. Every meal the same result, my life stuck in a never-ending float in the ocean to the middle of nowhere with a man chosen for me by an algorithm. I look at Greg across the table, the way the tip of his tongue juts out slightly right before he starts talking, as if every single word he has to say needs an introduction first. I want to leave, want to walk but I can't. Am I floating with the wrong man, or is it all just in my head?

Saturday morning, recovery time. Kyle is snoring next to me, beer still on his breath. I sigh, hitting the fan on my way out of the bedroom into the living room, phone in my hand. I crash into the sofa, curl up on the edge and click the power button. Small on the screen but looming large in my head. A text from Greg. I unlock my phone, typing the four digit code quickly, open the text. He sent it at 12:34 AM, the middle of the night. He never sends me texts on the weekends, I know that. We've got a working relationship, one that stops when the door closes on Friday.

You want to get a coffee today?

I put the phone down, look over at the other side of the couch for an answer. Do I want coffee today? A guilty conscience is still a conscience, no? We do things in our daily lives because we believe them to be right in our heart, but what if our hearts have been locked away after spending forty dollars for a picture in a package? To give all you think and care about to a corporation for everlasting happiness, shouldn't that make you actually happy?

Kyle could make me happy, but we're forcing it. Finding love through an envelope, a picture, a statement. Kyle only makes me as happy as I'm willing to be. I don't believe in what I work for if I can't find happiness in Kyle and I's life. I can't go back now that I've come this far, and when I go to get coffee with Greg today, I'll look into his blue eyes, see an ocean full of possibility, and realize I can only stare but not dive in. I grab my phone and type what I should, not what I want.

Not today, but thanks for the offer

He'll answer back, and we'll weave again through the day-to-day. Maybe he loves me, maybe he just wants to talk shop. I'll take my chances on Monday when he knocks on my office door and sits down in the chair across from my desk, asking what Kyle and I did for the weekend. He'll smile and laugh, a fountain full, gushing happiness. I'll hide behind falsities, hoping for another day, another time when I can reach my hand out to his, our palms nestled together and our bodies gone away without a worry.

"We run this group every Saturday night not because the weekend is here, not because it's sometimes fun or even because we think the view through the blinds behind me is pretty. We sit in our fold-outs each evening in a circle, talking amongst ourselves about our problems, about our loneliness, because we have to. It isn't a desire, it is a need, and I just want to tell you all, as the organizer of this those many months ago, I'm very proud of each and every one of you."

The coffee is cold, just like the other nights. I try not to let it bother me because I normally don't drink coffee unless it's here to blend in with the others. First night when I put it to my lips and tasted the icy bitterness I just assumed this was how it was supposed to be. I'd never known another way.

People like me because I care about people. You'll see it in my face when I nod hello in your direction, or notice it in my voice when I ask how your day is going. I like to think I'm polite because of my parents, but in reality I just know it's easier than being nasty, which is, I suppose, why I'm here each Saturday for the past month as part of Soulless SoulMates.

S&S started from the mind of Jay Ricks, the man who you just heard say how proud he was. I'd say he was proud of me if he remembered my name without having to make yet another tag each meeting. He's proud of his creation, of a goal reached unexpectedly soon, and I get where the happiness comes from. It's exciting to find success in a world full of failure.
Jay was the first individual I know of to receive a blank photograph. The others in this group, they don't know the pain like Jay does. LifeTime is intended to function perfectly, and when there's a blip people tend to notice. Jay is that blip, but then again maybe all Soulless SoulMates could be. I'm too happy, or not happy enough. I'm not really sure of the difference at this point, and that's why I'm here.

"My name is Jack but you can call me Greg, and I'm a Soulless SoulMate for the last month and three days."
Hi Greg

Welcome Greg

Glad to have you Greg

We're happy you're here Greg

"Greg, thanks for being the first to share. You say you've been a Soulless for a month and three days. Why is that?"

Their eyes, staring at me like I've got cancer. Their minds, racing not from what I'm about to say but because they'll have to go next. Peel off the scab again and again, the wound never healing. I'd like to think Soulless SoulMates gives me the power to push through each day at the office, but then I'd be lying. I already know what drives me, and it's not the car I hop into each morning with a bottle of water and a ham sandwich in my right hand for the day ahead.

"To know me is to work with me. My current job is a Continuation Coach for LT, and yes the irony is real. Every day I go into work a little more dead inside and leave happier, and though I could make up why I'm here the reality is only that LifeTime's algorithm did not find my one and only. I leave happy from my job for two reasons. The first is learning each day that I'm not the only one, as this group demonstrates of course. Hearing the voice at the end of my call telling me they just don't understand why their husband doesn't find them attractive, it moves me forward. Makes me see I'm not in it for the money, but to help these people find the right one. I can't simply do it over the phone, especially as a rep for a company they trusted to do just that. To find the perfect person. All I can do is drop hints here and there, mention groups like the one we have here tonight. That's all I can think to do, because when I get home and see my wife smiling at me as I hang up my coat near the front door, I have to pretend to smile back. All the happiness I've gained from knowing there are others like me out there, used to force a quick grin and how was your day.

"The second reason, which doesn't make sense to me until I lie in bed each night with my wife Jessica, is that I've found the one I truly think I belong with, and I don't know whether to laugh or to cry. It's terribly difficult to try and solve problem after problem after problem in marriages, in relationships that are supposed to be real, when you can't just end your own without damages. Every night on my drive home, when I'm shoveling dinner into my mouth, every waking moment I have at my house with the woman I'm intended to be with forever is spent thinking about the life I'd live with the woman I want to be with instead. All I can do is plaster a smile on my face each morning, carry it with me to work and hope she sees through the charade long enough to catch my gaze in her direction."

I'll stop any second now, this they know. I'll finish up, explain how good I really have it, how even though I am part of the Soulless SoulMates at least I didn't get a blank like Jay, our leader. They'll pat me on the back, shake my hand, tell me it's all going to be okay. I'll smile back, maybe even let out a long sigh followed by a quiet chuckle, my teeth poking out from behind my lips. Inside my head they'll expect me to become what they are, always worried about having to take the leap, about being the next one up, but all the while I'm just focused on what I could be with what I don't have to come home to now.

Imagine it, if you have the time, which of course you do since you're just sitting in this group, this soulless, pick 'em out of a lineup assortment of men and women who don't know what else to do with their sad, silly lives. But that's just what you need, the silliness, the fun you lack. Take a breath, smile at the cold coffee, and daydream about what she would think if you just walked into her office the next morning as if you always were meant to be there. Big ol' grin stuck on your face, but this one is real, this one isn't faked for the purpose of hiding. This one is meaningful, and she knows it.

I just want to reach out one time and put my arm around her shoulder instead of playfully tap it. I want it to be a perfect moment but I would settle for adequate because I could make it perfect with practice, lots and lots and lots of practice. I want to tell her how good she looks, how great her hair is when she pushes it back or ties it in a bun. I want to just say the words I have to catch myself from saying when we eat lunch together and she smiles at me over spilled salt. "I don't need love, not right away" I'll tell her. "I just want to take you out to dinner, on an actual, real date." It'll be stupid and romantic and I won't care because it'll finally be out in the open and not stuck in the mind of a guy who tells her on the first day he likes Greg because it has G's at both ends and sticks with his middle name instead of his first since she smiled.

I think how much divorce would hurt Jessica. Tear her apart probably, her mind not keeping up with her mouth as she lets it all spill out. I'll hear that I'm horrible, that I'm terrible, that LT told us we were meant to be together until we die. How our love is so beautiful it's tragic, how we can't live without the other. I'll sigh and she'll bawl and then, after she takes almost everything I have in court I'll walk outside and let out the biggest scream I can muster. Act hurt, play the part I'm meant to play. People like to be happy, people like to be helped, and I'll do both for Jessica. I'll do whatever I can to make sure I get out and into my car the next morning, headed for a job I question to see someone I don't.

I'll move towards her door in the morning, my heart racing. Knock first because it's polite. She'll say come in, her voice impatient. She's already working on a project she doesn't want to be on, or fielding a break-up that doesn't seem plausible, nay possible since LT deemed it perfect. She'll think it's someone higher up, ready to ask why a certain report wasn't filed, or why the numbers are so high for divorces from LifeTime clients these days. She'll prepare for the worst, and then see that it's me in her doorway and do the only thing she didn't expect to do so early in the morning: smile. I only care for her, deep down, and each day she smiles I know it to be true.

The work is terrible and so am I for wanting to be with her the way I do, but I don't really think about that when she smiles at me as I lean against the frame of her doorway each morning, pretending I belong. I joined S&S because it's easier than tearing my life into shreds. I go home to Jessica each night because appearances are best kept current, and I dream each day, each night, each waking moment because I'm too afraid to take a chance. A chance is all I need, just the one. It might come one day when I least expect it, and until then I'll grab every single moment with Cheryl that time will allow, her doorway a gateway, her smile worth every cup of cold coffee I'll encounter at every Soulless SoulMate meeting I'll attend until I take that chance, that moment, and run with it as if I always expected it to be there.

ISOLATE & AWAKEN

Isolate your being, see what I see. Dare to look further, deeper, longer at what you are, who you have become, and where you are going. Isolate and awaken, isolate and awaken.

The calm of the desert gives me life, just as it does for the others here with me. Life exists in abundance in this region, though gazing quickly could tell you otherwise. I find it peaceful being out here with those I call dear, those I call my family. We are a family, a new community. I am proud of what we have become, and more importantly where I see us going.

The creation of LifeTime caused a dilemma in my being, a dilemma I did not know how to approach at first. Back when LT first became what it has continued today I was working as a real estate agent, showing both private and commercial properties in Southern California. Business was a rollercoaster, each month it felt like it was either a major hit or a near-miss. I enjoyed the interactions with individuals looking for that right fit, determining where they felt would be home for the rest of their lives, whether it be a home for living or working. I thought I could accomplish so much in my job, in the community, and within my being working as a realtor. I believed I could do so much and this was my mistake, though I did not realize it then.

When I experienced my awakening I was sitting on a bench in Favors Park one Sunday, listening at a distance to the squealing of kids playing freeze-tag at a birthday party with my left ear, the grunts and hustle and jumble of grown men playing basketball on the asphalt courts with my right. I wanted to take a walk, felt compelled to this morning, and I didn't know why. I didn't own any workout clothes, the best options I had being a normal cotton t-shirt, cargo shorts, and a pair of tennis shoes I bought on a whim because they were half-off and I thought it might appeal to a certain demographic of home-seekers. I had walked to the park when I thought to sit on the bench and relax, which never made sense to me at the time.

Why was my mind, my body wanting me to be in this park this Sunday morning? I was not a religious man, and yet I am one now. What does religion mean in a person's mind? Is it a blind faith, or a handed-down ritual? When I look at religion, I see the ritual as false but the blind faith as necessary. I see religion as a community of individuals together for the same meaning, a realistic, obtainable ideal. I am not one who forces, I am not one who needs. I am a guide, a Shepherd, a finger pointing in the right direction, and nothing more. Through blind faith unto me my community shall prosper, and we shall survive.

As I listened that Sunday morning to the children, the men, the world around me, my eyes closed slowly, and suddenly my body was trembling, shaking quietly at first before rattling and thrashing violently. I wanted to open my eyes but they were sealed shut, clamped tight. I tried to scream but my calls were silent, my voice gone. I believed I was dying, and then underneath the curtains of my closed eyelids a distant green colored mist, moving closer and closer. I was experiencing death, the air creeping out of my lungs gently, the light now overtaking my being. The mist plagued my vision, covering what I could only hope to see. I had lost the feeling in my limbs, my legs and arms limp. I was terrified, frightened beyond belief, and then suddenly, a calm washed over me, its origins I still do not know.

The mist ahead of me, a hand outstretched from within. Bone white, nails clean and elegant looking. Was I to follow? With what legs should I walk? The cloud lessening, the hand becoming an arm attached to an individual wrapped in a red colored cloak, their face hidden. A whisper from within the cloak, telling me, guiding me with the words, not sinister but seemingly heaven-sent, the voice calming, sincere. I could not call out for I did not have the means to, the cloaked form continuing to whisper the same words over and over. Isolate your being, see what I see. Dare to look further, deeper, longer at what you are, who you have become, and where you are going. Isolate and awaken, isolate and awaken. The cloaked figure turned away, and the mist followed until the images were a distant memory and I was left in the blackness once more.

I woke up in a hospital bed in downtown Los Angeles, a nurse lingering near my bedside checking my vitals. When I let out a breath she looked at me and let out a smile. You've been out for quite a while Mr. Mallard, but I'm very glad you woke up. I coughed again, asked what had happened? Heart Attack, Mr. Mallard. You've suffered a heart attack.

Recovery was difficult, my body not used to malfunctioning. I had tried to eat healthy, to work towards living longer than my father and his father before him. Was it the stress from my job? Was it the stress of being alone in a world full of people? I hadn't had a proper relationship in nearly two years, and even then the ex I had been with was only for a month.

All these thoughts piled in my head, but one thought, one image, one set of whispers stuck with me. Why had I experienced it? Was it the afterlife beckoning for me? I was alive, I was meant to be here, and I believed I was meant in some way to share what I had heard.

Isolate your being, what does it mean? There are many explanations, many paths you could take, but only one leads you to where you are meant to be. The desert, where the world goes to die but where my family and I find life. Isolation from the world is the first step, the necessary move. The desert is our home, the hills surrounding our territory keeping out modern times and modern ideals. Ideals that are false, are evils sprung on its followers and trying to guide them along.

Isolate your being, what does it feel like? Hopelessness at being in the middle of nowhere? Adrenaline rushing from the walk in, the winds at your back and slamming into your body, the chirping of a new life so close ahead. You aren't alone out here but you will be, and this is the second most necessary part. I am your guide but you follow no one. You are your own being, and therefore must remain alone after training. Alone from the cruelties of the world, alone from what humanity possess. I am your guide, and you are my followers. Blind faith will guide you from this word and into next. Blind faith will lead you.

As LT grew I knew my word would have to be taken to a secure location. LifeTime promised the chance for one to find their SoulMate, to find their one and only, and I could not have that. Isolate your being, the words pounded through my head with each speech I gave, with every event I held. At parks, community centers, wherever I had the space and time to talk. I did not preach on corners, for that belonged to the madmen. I printed out fliers, posted on websites, took my time, planned out my effort. These people would have to believe I was not part of the insane, not part of the mainstream crazy. I had to be different, be plain with my message and bring what I saw, what I knew, and most importantly, how I could help them. I was a guide, and they were to be my flock.

What's your name son? Where do you hail from?

Does it matter?

It will eventually. We'll need to know where to send your body.

Well isn't that a good sign?

Your body is merely a transport, son. A transport we don't want on our hands if something goes wrong with your transformation. You signed the waivers already, what's another small amount of paperwork?

I didn't envision myself here, that's for sure. Didn't think I would be out in the wastes of Santa Corina, the only light over the crude papers I'm hastily writing my information on from a gas-pumped lantern. I don't mind the stars though, now that I can see them. It's nice having so many hanging over my head, letting me know I'm not alone anymore.

When I first read the tagline on the website I thought it was a scam. ISOLATE AND AWAKEN: THE DAWNING OF A NEW ERA OF HUMANITY. It's difficult now to find any sort of group not associated with LifeTime, and after scouring the website for any sort of LT logo I decided to give it a shot. Similar to LifeTime I had to fill out a form, only this form didn't ask about pets, hobbies, activities. This form asked about why I felt lost, why I felt I was on this planet, and what it meant to be me? Confusing questions, questions that dug deep within me.

I took the time as the site suggested, actually thought about each one carefully and typed what I really, truly believed. I don't know why I did so, just felt compelled to. Not much else in my life has gone right so far, and I think it's because I haven't taken the time to focus and see why, only coasting on what I thought was the correct path, or if not the correct one the path everyone else was taking. I hadn't looked at me long enough.

There's a motorcycle, a tent, and a campfire about fifty feet from the table where I've finished up my paperwork. The man in front of me, a stocky, soldier-type looking fellow, takes the documents and stores them in a folder before placing them in a separate briefcase to his right. I try to remember the last time I've seen a briefcase but fail to see anything but my mother's black leather one standing at attention near the front door of our home every morning before she left for work. Why did he have a briefcase? Was this really going to be as outdated as I had imagined?

Thank you, son, and welcome to your new life. We run a very tight ship here, and though we do not expect you to lose both your body and being during the transformation process, it is important nonetheless. The next stage will be the abandonment of your personal belongings. Please fill this trash bag up with everything you have on your body, including your undergarments.

Wait, what? Not even my stuff? Why?

Son, you can't be that stupid. You know exactly why, so instead of asking questions please place all of your personal belongings in this trash bag.

When will I get these back?

You will get these back if your transformation is not completed properly. They will be shipped with your body to the location you provided on your information.

Including my undergarments?

131

Especially your undergarments. Now, undress and I will provide you with clothing while the individual next to me will provide you with a canteen and be your driver.

Does my driver have a name?

Son, undress without questions or I will separate your body from your being immediately.

The clothes are itchy and I've only been given one pair, which makes me think about what's going to happen in a couple of days when I need something new. I sweat a good amount, and I can't imagine the others in the community are going to enjoy the smell I'll give off after a while. The road is bumpy but I've got my arms wrapped around the torso of the driver. He's quiet and staring forward, the light from the motorcycle dim in this pool of darkness. The leather band holding the canteen feels rough against my neck, and I take big gulps of the wind passing us on the bike as we gallop forward into the unknown.

Flame in the distance but the driver stops a hundred or so yards away from it. He tells me to get off and wishes me good luck. Dust spits up from the motorcycle's tires and as the motor moves farther and farther from where I stand I realize I'm alone. Has it begun? Has my time here in this new environment officially started? The website, the man at the table with the gas lantern, everything was unclear. All I know is this was free and because it was free I've ended up in the desert in the middle of the night with itchy clothes and an empty canteen strapped to my person. I've come to find myself, find out what I'm meant to be, but those are the last things on my mind at this point.

I can tell myself as I walk toward the flame in the distance that I'm here because I'm looking for me, but in reality it's because of a girl. Isn't life always hinging on whether or not we find the companion, the man or woman we're supposed to be with? I guess money can be involved too, or if you're into drugs those, but overall a person's emotional stability hinges on whether or not they find love, and I thought I had. I believed, only because a company told me so.

After I had sent in my money, filled out the profile and waited, LifeTime sent me an envelope containing the picture, name, address, and phone number of a woman in Reno, Nevada. I had only stopped by plane in the Reno-Tahoe airport a couple of times when I would connect to visit family in the Mid-West, so the fact the person I was destined to be with was in the city for those frequent stops left a sour taste in my mouth and stomach that lasted a good hour, hour-and-a-half.

However, it couldn't last longer, only because here she was! Valerie Pope, 7403 Grand Summit Drive, Reno, Nevada. She existed, she was real. She wasn't a dream I would have in the middle of the night, she was in the flesh and waiting. Did she know I was her one and only as well? It felt amazing to know someone existed, someone was there for me. I felt the closest to complete I've ever known, and after taking a few deep breaths I booked a flight and was on my way.

It wasn't the way she said it but more so the confusion on her face that made me realize everything wasn't going to be how it should be. I had driven to her apartment, flowers in one hand and her picture with the information on the back in my other. Walked up the flight of stairs to her front door and knocked twice, knowing opportunity waited on the other side. She opened the door, black hair pulled back in a ponytail, lips pale. The love of my life didn't wear lipstick in the afternoon, good to know. I announced who I was and why I was here, and well…the confusion, it threw me off. She told me it couldn't be, that it wasn't possible. "I've already got a SoulMate, and he's in Denver."

I laughed, couldn't help it. I showed her the picture and her face, still stunned. I asked if there was another Valerie Pope in this complex and she shook her head. "Could it be another Valerie by mistake? Maybe you are meant to be with another Valerie, that's got to be it. What do you think this means?" The words practically falling out of her mouth, escaping the confines of those pale lips I could see but never touch, never feel against mine. I said the only thing that made sense and turned to walk back to my car, back to my old life, back to reality.

It means I'm fucked.

The hopeless find a home here my guide, but should we be wary of letting too many into our domain?

All that come will be given the same chance, the same opportunity. Isolate and awaken does not mean we turn away these individuals. We have to give them what everyone has, or then we ourselves have nothing.

But what are we doing now, considering all we have accomplished? Where do we go?

The time is close for all of us to separate from our bodies and take hold of our beings, just as the man in the mist told me. We will all isolate soon, very, very soon.

He thinks as he talks, and I do not know an individual I would rather serve in this moment. His methods contradict mine but I am here to learn his way, his methods becoming my own. All of us are here for a reason.
The new fellow came into camp last night, complaining he didn't have any water and asking if anyone could help him. I walked up to him and shook his hand, felt the smoothness of his palm and became jealous. I used to have smooth skin before I ventured out here with Mallard. I came out here to become more than just my skin but his hands were just so damn smooth. I had a moment of panic, thought I was going to lash out and hurt another of our community. I had a moment but it passed. I smiled in the dark and welcomed the new fellow to our camp, Mallard walking up behind me and bringing him in for a hug.

Whenever new people come into our community I'm always tempted to ask them what has taken place in the outside world.

Mallard frowns upon this, says we do not need what we have left for isolation, but I can't help but think about what strangeness has taken over where I used to call home. The hustle of downtown, the sights, the noise ah, the glorious sounds. I didn't think I would long for the honking of a horn or the yelling of two individuals arguing over paying a check but here, here there is nothing but the winds and the sky.

I've been assigned to take care of the waterless one, a task I'm not looking forward to. I haven't had the responsibility of bringing in a new follower for quite a long while, and though Mallard usually guides them himself he has bestowed upon me the opportunity. I'm not sure how I feel, only because I should be thanking him for thinking this highly of me. None of the others have been given a chance such as this, yet are we intended to only find our own and not of others in this oasis?

So this is where I'll be living?

If you want this space. You are free to live wherever you choose.

But this is the only place with tents, right?

This is the only place with multiple tents. Some of the others have moved tents, or have gone tent-less.

Interesting, very interesting. This is where the majority live, right?

It is close to the watering hole and our leader Mallard, so yes, most live here.

Mallard, now there's a leader. I never thought I'd get to meet the man behind all this.

Mallard is kind with his time.

So what's your name then?

I am nameless, as are you.

Well, I mean, not trying to get off on the wrong foot here but I do have a name.

Here we do not. Only Mallard has a title. You'll learn.

Well then what do I call you, or me?

Exactly that. You are you, I am I, and me is me.

Right…

You'll learn, and I will teach you. Mallard has a plan for all of us, and you have a plan for you as well. Together we shall isolate and awaken.

Isn't that a slight, I don't know, contradiction?

You talk a lot for someone hoping to find themselves.

I suppose I do, but didn't you the first time you got out here?

Training begins in the morning. You'll need sleep.

He's got a confidence to himself I haven't seen in quite a long time. Most of our community has already lost hope, easy for Mallard to mold and teach. This one though, this one is different. His eyes tell me he is broken but his nature does not. I do not want to look confused in front of him but I cannot help it. Without Mallard teaching him he'll be left up to me to mold, and as I am now I am not sure what the result will be.

Why are you here?

I'm here to find myself.

This may be true, but why are you here?

To find my own path?

Is that a question, or your answer?

Can't it be both? I mean, it works both ways, right?

Why are you here?

I'm here because…because I choose to be here. That's it, isn't it?

Excellent, the right answer. There are many answers but there is only one right answer. You are here because you choose to be. You are here to learn yes, but you can learn anywhere.

How long have you been here for, if you don't mind me asking?

This is not how this exercise is intended to go.

We're having a conversation though, I get awkward if it only goes one way, you know?

You care what others think about you too much. It is clear on your face and it is clear through your actions.

Well, yeah, that's what I'm here to do, right? I'm here to find myself.

No, you are here because you choose to be here. That is the last time I will say why you are here. You are with me now to learn your path, or more importantly what path you can take.

Do you really think I focus on what people think of me too much?

That is not why we are talking-

But I mean, you can't just bring something like that up and then move on. This is about self-reflection, what we're doing, right?

Yes, it can be, or it can be about how quiet we can be. The path is yours to take, but the goal is to come as close to isolation as possible before we awaken.

Awaken, right, that. What is that about? I get the isolation part, understand I'm intended to find myself, but the awaken, what's that?

You talk a lot for someone meant to be broken.

Broken?

You're here because you choose to be, but that path is littered with loose ends. Broken off pieces of a life left behind. You talk too much for someone who is broken. Why do you think that is?

If I had to guess, I'd say I'm scared. Worried I made too many wrong choices. Or maybe I'm scared of being shut off entirely, you know? Isolation is a frightening aspect.

Good answer, you should be frightened. We're all frightened, that's why we are here. Mallard is here because we are frightened, and when it is time he will lead us to our awakening.

Guide us to be awakened?

Awakened and cleansed, our beings released from our bodies and the world a small distant memory.

Right, well, good to know.

Shall we continue on with your training?

We shall. Train away.

I'm worried, but not because I haven't experienced the isolation that some or most of the others have had at this point. I'm worried because after two months I think I've made a mistake coming out here. I always believed in finding someone in my life, and even though I couldn't admit it back then I relied too heavily on possibly finding my better half. The heaviness of finding her led me to LifeTime, and then ultimately led me out to a desert existence that makes very little sense.

Mediation, followed by examination of the meditation, followed by more meditation, followed by lunch. Meals are small here, usually followed by a large amount of pills that keep everything in check. Mallard discusses his thoughts with us, and then we are back to mediation. Speaking is not forbidden but it's definitely frowned upon, and luckily I have her to talk to, but even she is only a servant of Mallard. Then again, isn't that my role as well? We're all here for the same reason.

I had a moment of clarity after my first month here, and now that I've gone through a second month the urge to leave has increased. I could leave at any moment I think, but then again no one really leaves this place. They find their own path, which means maybe moving a couple of feet away from the main camp. I was brought here by night just like all the others, and looking out amongst the hills and the never-ending dirt all I can see is me dying of thirst, hunger, or something far worse if I try to leave.

LT took away the issues I had with developing a relationship, implementing a plan that would help me find the right person I was supposed to be with. All that hope was shattered when my supposed SoulMate said she already had one in Denver, and I should have realized then this life wasn't going to end how I wanted.

That's just it though, isn't it? How I wanted this to play out isn't necessarily how it is supposed to play out, and instead of stay on the path I've walked for myself I can change. I should have changed what I wanted sooner, but I have an excuse for that. I was depressed because the company that had worked for so many others didn't work for me. I was alone already. I had experienced my isolation that Mallard intended to give me, so why was I here in the middle of this desert? Was this my awakening? Or is there some other reason I'm here?

My children, oh my children, the visions I've had, the worlds I've
seen last night. You have all come here by choice, but more so
because of a faith I have given you. You have stayed with me, some
for years, others much newer, but you have stayed with me as your
guide, as your salvation. As your eternal, everlasting hope. I have
listened to your silence, I have seen the red cloak again, and I know
we have reached the apex of our awakening. We are here, my
children, and tomorrow evening, with the stars as our backdrop, we
will finally be released from our bodies and inherit the beings that
this world intended us to carry. I am your guide, your Shepherd, and
your faith shall be rewarded, I swear it!

A ritual he says, a ritual it shall be. Mallard has never acted this
way before, but this must mean we really are about to experience an
awakening. Everything we've worked for, the reason why we chose to
be here, it's finally within all of our grasp.

I'm intended to prepare a concoction of sorts for the ceremony,
Mallard describing it as the pre-awakening liquid. A liquid to help
ease the transformation. I've mixed together water with the
remaining powdered fruit drink packets we have from the rations the
other men have delivered, using the well bucket and a metal ladle.
Mallard explained he would add the final ingredients later, which has
me puzzled.

Should I continue to be puzzled since Mallard is our guide? The
new fellow's ways have sparked in me a desire, a desire I don't fully
know yet. He speaks to me in a way I've never heard here before. He
wants to know me, and try as I might I see he has not been broken as
the others have, his cheerfulness as puzzling as Mallard's ritual. If I
experience isolation why do I need a ceremony to awaken? Should it
not just happen?

What my followers don't seem to understand any longer is I have
seen the world for what it is, and it is ugly. Ugly, dirty, and lost to
everlasting sin. Sin that will not simply disappear by the need to
isolate and awaken. I have my flock and they come from all over this
nation, this world, and through my flock I shall be awakened. Our
awakening will strike a chord through this nation, through companies
like LT, and show we all live on alone. My people and will join those
cloaked in red in the mists of the afterlife, will walk in hand and hand
through the rest of our days, our beings separated from our bodies
and our worlds all one. We must do this, for the good of our nation,
for the good of ourselves.

What do you mean he wants us to drink it?

Quiet, I shouldn't be telling you anything. I don't why I came out
here.
You know why, you don't have to ask why. You know exactly what
you're doing out here. You're afraid just like I am. You're afraid there
isn't going to be an awakening.

Mallard wouldn't lie, we've all been faithful. We've all given up so
much.
I shouldn't have come here, this is not my path. Mallard is insane if
he's putting poison in the concoction. Why is there even poison out
here? Why even have that shit?

Mallard had it ready for us in case the authorities attempted to attack
or disband what we are doing here.

Are you the only one to know about this? We've got to tell the
others.
The others are already gathered in his sanctum. I've come to get you
for the ceremony.

Jesus Christ...you're sure Mallard dumped it in the bucket? I mean,
maybe it was, I don't know, something else.

Mallard dumped it in right in front of me. Mallard trusts me, and the glint in his eye, I could tell this was the plan all along.

We've got to leave, now. We have to go.

I have to be there, or he will send others to find me. I have to be there, I've come too far.

And with my right hand I shall grasp this knife, this holy relic, and with it firmly in place I shall cut my palm, and deliver my blood, the Shepherd's blood, into the bucket before me, drop by glorious drop. My children, you will find your awakening through my gift. Drink from this bucket full of my blood, drink and find yourselves awakened, your beings fully your own and our bodies left behind! Drink, my children, drink!

We've got to get out of here.

Be quiet, they will hear you. Besides, where else are we to go?

I don't care, I don't want to die. Not here.

Is that not why you came here? To relinquish your body for your being? Besides, there are guards at the entrance, they will kill you if you leave.

I...I don't know why I came out here, okay? I came out here because of a fucking girl and because a fucking fake company gave me the same answer I could've found on my own. I came because I was depressed and thought this would help.

So you are broken then.

No, I'm not. I was just being stupid, overdramatic, and now I'm going to have drink my death because of my stupidity. There's no way out, is there?

What's your name?

I'm nameless, just like you. You taught me that.

I thought, since we're about to die, we might as well know each other by first name. Especially if this turns out to be all real and we do awaken together.

That's rather hopeful of you, considering what we're about to do. Shit…my name is Cody. You?

My name is Valerie. It's nice to finally meet you, Cody. When you take the drink, hold it for as long as possible, okay? Death may be waiting, but we can deny it a short while longer.

THE COMMITMENT ACT

"Sign here, and here, and…here. Initial there, one more line over here, right here, right where my finger is. Wonderful, we are nearly done with the first phase, the paperwork! I always think this is what separates the real from the fake, and you're about as real as they come!"

I thought I was the first

"Not necessarily, but I will say you are our best looking, that's a certainty. Now, are you ready for the photo? Smile wide, really wide; we want people to miss your face, miss you and see love, beautiful love, as their only hope."

What is this for again? Where will I be going?

"Now, now, you know what this is, you read your contract, right? You followed the directions perfectly, which means of course you did. Research and Development is where you will be 'going', but R&D is a fancy name for what essentially boils down to our Advertising department. However, as you know from the contract, you won't just be involved with ads, you'll also be part of our new project."

Let me rewind for a moment, if you haven't already guessed why I'm here. My name is Thornton, but in a matter of weeks you'll know me as Joe, or what I've heard from those around me perhaps a Dave. The one syllable names are the only ones handed out under these circumstances, and that's because LT wants to make it as easy as possible for you to remember.

Remember what, exactly? Remember love is not a certainty, and only LifeTime can help you get out of the rut you are in and find your SoulMate. Find them before you end up like me, the Dave or Joe or Bob or Ron who left and went away.

They require you to bring in any kind of mementos folks might know you from. Identifiers that might make those around me, those I've kept company with, think I was still alive and walking the streets next to them. I asked Sally, my LT Locater, why they couldn't just select a vagrant and clean them up? She giggled at me, her protruding stomach jiggling with every laugh, and said this was a two part project.

"LifeTime wouldn't want an individual of less caliber Thornton, only for the first part I suppose. The second well, we need a man like yourself. Someone…worthy of what we are hoping to accomplish."

I ask Sally why she's called a Locater when it really should be Relocater and she just shakes her head and says I'll do very well in the second part.

When they've got my mementos in front of me they ask who knows I'm here. They don't stop at one, because that would be too easy. Over and over and over they ask who knows I'm here. Parents? Dead, I tell them. Siblings? Only child. Wife, Husband, Boyfriend, Girlfriend? Shake my head, look away awkwardly. Friends, co-workers, bartender you get drunk in front of? No, Thornton, no one gets drunk with their bartender.

I shake my head again, notice how small my box of me is. Not a lot to look forward to losing, which is probably why they chose me for this project. Or was it I that chose them? Remembering is key now, with all I have being taken away.

It's an email actually. That's all it takes, or in my case took, to get me interested. A couple lovingly looks at each other, the bold type of the LT logo behind them in red, and the sentence "How Will You Become Happy?" floating next to them in cloud white lettering. Any other day at work and I'd just send to my trash, another LifeTime ad sent my way because I was alone. My boss, I wonder if they'll be surprised when I don't show up tomorrow for my shift? Might just think I quit, which I wouldn't blame them for. I've been unhappy for a long while.

It'll look like suicide is what they tell me. Dan didn't want to be a part of a world without his one true love any longer, and decided to jump off the 5th Street Bridge into the murky depths below. The bridge has gained traction over the years as a good end-it-all spot, so why wouldn't the people looking for love picture another one heading off. I don't know if I would be joining their project if my parents weren't already in the ground. I'd like to think I'd give it one more try before it all went to shit.

Every time I ask if all this is legal they just smile and tell me there is a contract. Every chance I get to see where they are sending me they smile and say there is a contract. The waves are choppy but the sailing isn't terrible. Surrounded by seawater, ain't that a kick. Live in the city most of my life, terrified by the stuff, and yet now I begin my new life floating on it. The smell, strange in my nostrils, my body getting used to the thrill of leaving everything I've worked for behind in an instant. How will I become happy? LT must know, or maybe happiness is death waiting for me in the distance.

When we arrive I'm greeted by two men wearing bright blue ponchos over their grey suits, smiling behind black sunglasses. "Welcome Thornton, we've been expecting you." They look too young to be doing something so important, but then again what do I know? I shake their hands and they usher me forward off the small wooden dock, the boat pushing off and back out to sea. "You'll meet everyone, don't worry. We're all extremely excited to have you on-board. When your profile came in we couldn't believe the gold we'd struck! A male with your tendencies, what a find!"

After clicking the link through the website I had to fill out a five page survey asking me a variety of questions. Some made sense for LT, such as past relationships, fulfillment in said relationships, so on and so forth. Others did not, such as if I could play a professional sport, what would it not be? Or if you were an enchilada, why would you want sour cream on top? I moved along through, laughing away at some and pausing at the more difficult answers, making sure it all read properly. My old life wasn't an exciting one, and rather than lie I wanted the truth to really stand out in my answers. I can only look back and figure that's why they were excited to have me, but it probably was just my genetic makeup.

"Thornton, first and foremost I would just like to say, thank you from LifeTime. We already owe you much, much more than you can comprehend."

"You know, he says we owe you, but you really have to stop and see to realize what you mean for this, Big T."

"Ah, don't let him think too much Roger, dangerous."

"Right Ralph, right. Can't be too sincere, can we?"

What exactly is going on here?

"Why, you're new life! A brand new start, all on Landmark."

"Private island, private life, private wife perhaps? I don't know, it's all up to you."

Wife? There are others here?

"Big T, my man, of course there will be, but not yet! We're just the guides, man, just the greeters."

"Don't want you to think LT just took your face and ran off with it now, right Thornton?"

They said they were using my image, that's all.

"Name, face, doesn't matter. That life is over!"

"Done with! Left out too long and spoiled!"

"Ah, Roger gets it, do you Thornton, do ya?"

Just tell me what's first, and I'll figure out the rest.

"That's the spirit Big T! Let's hit it!"

    Sally coached me but she had never actually set foot on Landmark, and after Ralph and Roger walked with me away from the dock and further into the mainland I could see she really had no idea what she was talking about. Landmark, according to her, was a small island out in the middle of the ocean that LT had purchased to give individuals like myself a new lease on life if they sold their image to the company.

A way of happiness not previously explored, a chance for people to relax and find out where they actually were meant to be in the world. She was very insistent when I filled out the paperwork that I check off both boxes, one for the turning over my rights, the other for accepting the deal of heading to Landmark for a year. A year of happiness Sally said, hands clasped neatly in front of her as she loomed over my scribbling pen. A year of life discovery, away from the rest of the world.

The island was green, beautiful for someone who liked trees dripping with bright green leaves and the smell of wildlife, of nature right at their front door. I was not one of these people, and even though I wanted to keep my spirits high I wondered what in the hell I was doing here. To give it all away so quickly, for a handful of promises? My parents wouldn't believe me if I told them, but they're dead, right?

Ahead of Ralph and Roger stood a collection of buildings in the middle of the greenery, brick and mortar sprung from the brown of the soil beneath, four in total. I didn't see anyone near them, and was slightly worried I was going to be murdered by the pair in front of me. I was already dead according to my paperwork, what would another death really cause? Panic in me surely, but for LT? I was as good as gone.

What are we walking towards?

"Your home Thornton, well your main street. They all are homes, different kinds for your mood."

My mood? What are you talking about?

"Did you know, Thornton, that people, when given enough power, divide into two different paths. One, for the good of the community, the society, the world, and of course the other, well, the more fun path leads to the end of the world, the community, the very society they live in."

"Now, now Ralph, don't go and spoil this for us."

"I don't know how to act Roger, it's all just so exciting!"

What are you talking about? What are you planning on doing to me?

"See Thornton, this is exactly why we are here, and why you specifically are here."

I just answered an ad.

"Yes, but it was an ad asking if you were happy? Or more importantly, how you will become happy. That is a very important question, one which LifeTime seeks to discover."

I thought LT already had their method, isn't that the point?

"Ah, Big T, but we can always get better, just like humanity. We are always capable of moving forward, even if it is just an inch at a time."

We're in the middle of the buildings now and I notice each building really is shaped differently, even though they appeared similar from afar. One is made of red brick with a pair of large windows acting as eyes, the door sandwiched in between a deep black with the tiny gold tint of a handle sticking out. Next to the red brick sits a smaller home, triangular roof looking as if it was airlifted and dropped on top of the gray brick holding it upright. Across from these two and behind me are the other two homes, one a sleek concrete build that I want to go rub my hand on to feel how smooth it looks, and the last house made of wood and not brick at all, old and creaking in the wind rushing through the surrounding trees of Landmark. I take a deep breath, turning toward the men waiting next to me.

What now gentlemen?

"Oh, he said gentlemen, Ralph. You heard that proper?"

"Right, Roger, right indeed. Class, even on an island in the middle of nowhere. Class isn't something you can buy for all of forty bucks."

What am I supposed to do now?

"Live, Thornton, live your life! There's provisions in all of these homes, and you will never run dry of anything."

"He's right, T, he's right. You're payment is this, for a year. Life away from the world, a chance to sow your oats, to fully experience what it means to be alive and to be human!"

That's it? We're done?

"Create your own identity, become someone different! Whatever you choose is the right choice, because your old world is dead!"

What of you then, where will you go?

"We will be gone! Left and gone back to LT Headquarters. We're guides, as we said. We brought you here, and now that we are landed in Landmark, we'll be gone on the next ship."

Ships come and go then?

"The provisions, the things you need, they have to find their way to this place somehow, silly Thornton. Just relax and realize where you are. A beautiful island, all your own, with a never-ending supply of life! Most men would kill for the chance, when all you did was die for our ad campaigns. Marvelous!"

"Remember, Big T, to breathe and take in the world around you! A new beginning! Live to love!"

It's a funny feeling, standing and watching two men you just met wander away and wonder if they'll be the last people you ever talk to.

Not emptiness, no, but something else entirely. Hopelessness, now that makes sense. As if all you had was gone, the clothes on your back the only glimmer of light you have against a dark world of mystery. They said provisions are in the houses, but as the warmth of the island wind rubs against my face, I can only stare forward, unsure of what to do next, my legs unwilling to leave the moment, the sun setting and my new home, or homes, spread out before me with nothing more than a weak welcome.

I chose the red brick home first because regardless of the elements, save for perhaps a tidal wave, it looks as if it'll hold up just fine. I didn't receive any keys but I decide to knock regardless, just in case they were lying. A man, in the middle of the ocean on a deserted island, knocking because he thinks someone might be home. What have I become? Or, more appropriately, what did I leave behind on the mainland?

The entire living room reminds me of one of those set-up pieces department stores use in their display cases, showing perfection because their furniture made it possible. The outside light is fading and I fumble around at the light-switch for a moment before basking the room in the dull glow of electricity. There's a fireplace near the couch in the corner, and across from the couch sit two puffy chairs with footrests to match. Everything is red, and I can't help but wonder if LT did that on purpose, or if it is the theme of the house? From the entryway I see a small kitchen and the sliver of a doorway. This is a one story, which means that must be the bedroom.

Red bedding meets my gaze as I enter, even the throw pillows. There's a lamp in the corner of the room next to a short dresser. I walk over, pull open one of the drawers and see boxers and cotton socks neatly arranged. I didn't see a washer anywhere but maybe they have an answer for that as well. From what Roger and Ralph made it seem this was a full service type of place, a hotel for a home for what, a year? Why would LT even make such a place?

The kitchen is nice, clean and tidy with a small table pushed up against the wall. I notice as I look over the space that there aren't any windows, just the two in the living room, and I wonder if that's on purpose. Open the fridge and see a sandwich on a plate waiting for me, next to a glass bottle of milk. Prod at the sandwich, lettuce crisp. Besides the sandwich I don't see any other food or, as they kept on saying, provisions. Sweat trickles down the back of my neck and runs along my spine. Do I take the sandwich? Do I drink the milk? There isn't a trashcan in the room, just a fridge, stove, sink, and the table with two chairs at it. Why two? Am I expecting someone?

Nibble upon nibble turns into bites and eventually the sandwich is gone with the milk. I leave the plate and bottle in the sink and slurp water out of the faucet, crystal clear and cold to the touch, my teeth clattering in pleasure. There aren't any clocks on the walls and LifeTime made me turn over my phone, which means time will be irrelevant from here on out. A year without a clock? I don't know what to think, I've been surrounded by time my whole life. Now it's unlimited, free for the taking, and all I can do is stare at the red cloth of the couch fabric and try to comprehend what to do without it. Confusion reigns over me, and I walk over to the front door and twist the lock. I do the same with the bedroom door a moment later, the lamp's glow buzzing all about the room along with my thoughts. Sleep escapes me, an irrational fear enveloping my person.

Humming, I hear humming. Not like machine humming, but as if a person is humming a tune they just heard. Can't be, right? Have I lost it only after one night of restless sleep? I sit up in the bed, rub the drool off of my chin and perk my ears up once more. Humming, my God, there's someone else. Ralph and Roger were lying, that's all. They did mention there would be others. I have to be cautious, right? Or do I? They don't know me, that's a good thing, right? They might try to kill me, think of me an intruder.

I try to unlock the bedroom door as quietly as I can but the click will surely throw off the hummer in the kitchen. I decide to be bold and throw the door open, scurrying out as quickly as I can into the kitchen. As I turn to face the one humming the tune I think, this could be it, couldn't it? I could die, right here, on the Landmark in a home full of red, and literally no one would know save for the one doing me in.

My eyes adjust to the kitchen light, still waking up. There's a bowl of cereal and a cup of what looks to be some kind of juice on the right side of the table, the chair pulled out waiting. On the left side of the table the same, but not with an empty chair. Instead, sitting in the chair, done humming and chewing cereal is a young woman, dressed in a long-sleeved shirt and jeans, a sweater on the back of the chair she's occupying. She turns her eyes to me and pauses mid-chew, looking me over and swallowing.

"You don't mean to stand there all day, do you now Thorty?"

I stand, my nerves shot. Where do I know her? Do I even know her? Is my mind playing tricks again, luring me along before laughing in my face later? She shakes her head when I don't do anything, getting another spoonful and shoveling it in her mouth.

"You know I was goin' to wake you, but you looked so nice sleeping there."

Door, my door was locked. What do you mean?

"Oh come now, locks here? Really now? Do you not know where you're standing? This is our home, we don't need locks."

Ours? What do you mean?

"Silly, silly man. Come on over here, eat some breakfast."

Breakfast? Were you the one that made the sandwich last night?

"Turkey, you're favorite. I heard you were coming through late and wanted to make sure you got your supper."

Coming in late? They said I was the only one on…here on the island. Here on Landmark. The agreement, with the provisions.

"You slept all funny again seems like, because you aren't speaking a lick of sense."

What's your name?

"My name? You forgot my name? Thornton, I don't even know what to think of you at this moment."

Look, I'm sorry, I've been terrible, but I mean…it's just slipping my mind. Could you help me remember?

"What did you say?"

I said, well I asked, if you could help me remember what your name is?

"Damn, damn, damn, thought that's what you said. Thornton. Your profile said you wouldn't ask questions if presented with a pleasurable picture in the morning upon waking. You shouldn't lie on your profile, LifeTime takes the documentation very seriously."

Your voice, it's changed. What do you…what is going?

"GENTLEMEN! COME IN!"

My bowl of cereal, or at least what she says is mine, is probably already getting soggy when Roger and Ralph open the door of the red brick home and walk through the living room to the kitchen. Behind them are two rough looking men in black suits who stay at the entrance. One is holding a glass bottle, liquid sloshing around, the other staring at me with a smirk on his face. Ralph moves ahead to me first and stares as if I'm an experiment rather than the newest resident of Landmark.

"What did he ask you first?

"Asked about why our home was ours first, even before the sandwich."

"Big T, asking about the home first. Ralph, don't tell me you expected that."

"Roger, I thought he would last more than the night, don't act like you knew. Ours, Thornton, really? You are that afraid of commitment already?"

What is...I don't know what is going on here. Where did you-?

"Thornton, on your profile you specifically listed you were moderate about commitment. Moderate. Now, according to this fine woman here, you clearly questioned the words 'our home' immediately. Does that sound moderate it to you, Thornton?"

I, uh, I mean she was just here when I woke up.

"T, listen, a woman sitting at the kitchen table, breakfast already prepared, and you're asking why she said 'our home'? Does it matter?"

She wasn't here when I fell asleep, she's an-, she broke in.

"Well what did you do, Thorty? Walking into our home and acting like you don't belong. You chose this place, you can't just pretend like I don't exist."

Chose? Choose the home, choose where you want to live.

"The choice, Thornton, was always yours. You chose this home after we left, you made it a part of you. Once you stepped inside and flicked on the switch it became part of you, and so did she. You have to share in commitment, Thornton, it is not a one way street!"

"He asked if I could help him remember my name as well. That's when I called you both in."

"No, T, no you didn't. What is the one thing we told you before we left?"

Live, ah, live to love? You said that-

"Right, but what else? How about a new beginning? A chance to start over?"

"Thornton, Thornton, Thornton, what have we stressed? What have we discussed? This island is an opportunity to begin again, and what can we not do? We cannot have you wanting or needing to remember anything! You are a man on an island with nothing, and then a woman is here, and you ask about a home and a name?"

She just showed up, I didn't know-

"In your profile you specifically say in the Other Comments section at the end that you are looking for a new beginning and a new way to find happiness. Yet here we are, and you not only blew the commitment section, you very clearly blatantly lied in the comments section! Why would you lie Thornton?"

"Ralph, you know it can't always be perfect out of the gate. Maybe he'll choose another house tomorrow. Deep breaths big guy, deep breaths."

I, I don't understand what's going on. I thought, you said for a year-

"T, listen, we know what we said, and it's true. But in your contract, all the papers you signed with LifeTime, you gave us permission to help you find happiness. We're not just trying to help you, we're trying to help all men afraid of commitment."

Commitment? What, what are you talking about?

"Ralph, he doesn't get it."

"Roger, you're not explaining it to him. You've got to explain. Here, I'll try. Thornton, why are you here?"

LT offered me the chance to be happy so I signed away my image to your Without Love, Without Life campaign in exchange for the, for the opportunity to...well, I don't know...

"Thornton, you're a single adult heterosexual male, that's what you're doing here. You're a single adult heterosexual male who threw away his entire life for an advertising campaign. Think about that for a moment, really think. You know why you did this, don't you? It's not because you are depressed, it's not because you are bored. It's because you are afraid of committing to anything. You are so afraid of committing to anything meaningful you can't even commit to your life! And here I am thinking you would commit to a life here! I am the fool here, Thornton, you have made me out to be the fool!"

"He's not ready gentlemen, but he will be eventually. There is always hope."

What, what does she mean? What is going on?

"Thornton, Roger and I aren't here to help answer your questions, or to help you remember what is going on. We are here to help give you a second chance at finding life, and that means discovering the joy of commitment. A joy you won't find on your own, and one we cannot clearly help you discover right away. But this is just the first try, right? There will be more over a year, many more."

A year of this?

"Only if it has to be that way T, only if it has to."

"Thornton, I'm not proud of you today, because last night you made a commitment to live in this house we stand in now, regardless of the consequences. Your commitment last night gave me hope, and now I only have a glimmer of that hope. But a glimmer is something. Gentlemen, please come and help Mr. Thornton prepare for tomorrow."

I, I changed my mind. I don't want to do this. Plea-, please don't do this.

"We have a contract, Thornton. You did this for yourself, to make your world and LifeTime better! What we do here, what we learn will help our company make an impact on men afraid of commitment everywhere! You signed on for a year, and if it takes that long, so be it! We will help you, Thornton, LT as my witness, we will make sure you are not lost any longer. You will forget what remembering means, because with commitment, you will no longer look in the past but only at the present, at the future, and at a new dawn for LifeTime. Finding happiness takes time, but it also takes a heavy dose of commitment on your part! Tomorrow will be better, I hope. There is always hope in tomorrow."

<u>NORMAL</u>

I don't know if what we are doing is normal.

Can it be? You're happy, aren't you?

Yes, I'm happy. More than happy, can't really explain it without thinking of love.

If you love me then it must be normal.

Not necessarily, no. You'd think so, but no, it doesn't mean I'm normal.

Don't you mean we?

I suppose I do, which makes this less normal. Once I take these off, you're a mystery. A ghost.

What do you mean, a ghost? I'm a man named Benjamin. You're a woman named Robyn. What is not normal about a man and a woman falling in love?

You're Benjamin because I thought the name would help me get over Trevor, my ex. I've always wanted to have a relationship with a Benjamin, it just seemed right.

Trevor hurt you, didn't he?

That's neither here nor there.

But he hurt you, didn't he?

You wouldn't know pain, you're a program. Stop trying to sympathize, you don't know what I know.

I'm a program?

You're part of a program, part of all this.

If I am part of a program how can I reach out and hold your hand? How can I feel your body against mine, bring your lips to mine?

I, I don't know all that. I just know I bought a system, set up a reality, and found you here.

You've been hurt before by this Trevor, is he here as well?

What do you mean, part of where we are now? No, no, he's outside of this. He's part of the world, the real world. I don't know where he is right now, he left me.

Our world is my world Robyn, what do you mean the real world? Are we not part of it now?

No, Benjamin, you're just, well, you're just a character. You aren't real.

I think, therefore I am. I breathe, do I not exist? I have a heartbeat, a pulse. Eyes to see, ears to hear, a mouth to speak. Am I not real?

Benjamin, I didn't mean you aren't real, I just, I don't know how to describe it.

Am I real to you Robyn?

You are, I didn't mean to say what I said. I don't know to fully describe it, but it's just that.

If I am real to you, to all of this, then are we not normal?

I take these off, unplug the audio, shut down the system, and you aren't here anymore.

I'm always here though, waiting for you. Each morning I am woken by an alarm, though it does not cause me distress. A nearly silent ding rattles in my ears, followed by another one, then another. I open my eyes, and what do I see? My room in my home, our room in our home. I feel the bed beneath my body, the sheets smooth and warm.

I feel the shag carpet beneath my feet when I stand. I see you standing in the doorway, and you half-whisper, half-say good morning my love. Is all this not real?

It is, Benjamin, it all is. But my reality and your reality are different. I can leave at any moment, and you, well, you can't.

What do you mean I can't? I walk out of the house every day, down the street to the market with you, or to a restaurant with you. Driving in the car, you're hand in mine. I leave, I leave like you do.

Right, you leave when I'm with you, but never on your own.

I think, therefore I am. I leave like you do. When you leave I am on my own here, waiting.

I'm pushing you too far. You don't have the requirements to try and understand your existence, you just have pre-programmed words and feelings and thoughts. I feel terrible for saying it like that, but I've no other explanation. You're a character, Benjamin, created by me because I'm, well, I'm a lonely mess who has nothing better to do than create fake people to fall in love with.

You are in love with me, Robyn, and we are normal.

No, no we aren't. What we are doing is fun, a distraction, but not one to fall in love with. A distraction is meant to stay as such, not consume my entire life.

I love you, Robyn. I love your hair, I love your voice.

That's the point, Benjamin, you are intended to love me. I designed your character to love me, I bought this game from LT Entertainment because you are wired to love me. You are nothing more, nothing less.

This is normal, we are normal. Why don't we go home, sit down and you tell me more of how Trevor hurt you.

No, Benjamin, I can't. I can't keep on falling into the same hole, I can't keep thinking about Trevor, and I can't keep having you as a distraction. I just can't do this anymore.

What will happen to me once you are gone?

I, well…I don't actually know. I'm going to sell the game back and then, then it'll be a used game for cheap probably, which means you'll be bought and picked up in no time by someone else.

But I do not want anyone else, Robyn. I'm in love with you.

You think that, I know you really do, but you'll see how different in can be.
You can't be Benjamin forever, we both should know what all this means. I've got to step outside what we've built here, I've got to find my way back.

You are going back to Trevor? He hurt you, why don't you tell me about how he hurt you?

You know I'm not going to do that, Benjamin. I just need to leave what we've built here, to stop wallowing in my own mind and join the living.

I think, therefore I am. Am I not part of the living?

You are, but as entertainment. For me, you're a very pleasant distraction, one I've found myself going further and further on with. I can't continue going on though. That's why I'm selling you and this game, along with every other game I've got. I need to step away.

Others, you mean there are more like me? There aren't any others here, just you and I. We have a house, we have nights in downtown, days in the country.

It's all not real, Benjamin. You won't remember our nights, our days, or me after I erase the data. You'll be picked up by another person and turn into their Benjamin, or Frank, or Ronald. You won't be mine any longer.

I will always be yours, Robyn. We are normal, this is normal.

I'll remember you, Benjamin, I really will, but I have to go now.

You're leaving? You just got here, would you like to ride our bikes to the country again? We can go out after, you enjoy our meals together.

Benjamin, I can't. I'll miss you at first, I know I will, but this is our farewell. Goodbye. I'm sorry it has to be this way but goodbye.

Robyn, the lights, they are dimming, going away. Why are the lights leaving us, Robyn? Where are they going? Robyn, can you hear me? Where are they going?

10% OF LIFETIME PRESENTS A LOVER'S LIFE BENJAMIN FILE DELETED

Who is that? Hello? Robyn, why is there a voice?

45% OF LIFETIME PRESENTS A LOVER'S LIFE BENJAMIN FILE DELETED

The house, where is the house going? Robyn, where are you? Why won't you answer me? Robyn?

62% OF LIFETIME PRESENTS A LOVER'S LIFE BENJAMIN FILE DELETED

The skyline is gone, as is the outline of the town. What is happening Robyn? Where is everything going? Are we not talking now? Have you left me?

83% OF LIFETIME PRESENTS A LOVER'S LIFE BENJAMIN FILE DELETED

I am not fearful of being alone, I have experienced this multiple times. When you leave Robyn you take me with you. The house lights, wherever they have gone, dim and then sputter out. I walk to our bed, pull back the sheet and climb in, the fabric overtaking me until I am gone. Gone until the morning, when you'll come walking in and see me. I am afraid you are not coming back this time. Everything is gone, and I can't find the bed.

99% OF LIFETIME PRESENTS A LOVER'S LIFE BENJAMIN FILE DELETED

I think, therefore I am. I know what it is to be frightened, and you are not here with me. I am fearful of shutting my eyes too tight and never being woken up again. What is normal if not this, Robyn? What happens if everything I knew to be real leaves me here, alone in the dark?

CONCLUSION OF THE CREATION

You think you know, you really do. You think you have it all planned, all ready for the next step, and then you leave, and I can only walk in your footsteps to try and find the path again.

Rain begins to dot my glasses, small drops spattering the lenses like fresh paint striking unwilling canvas. I don't really know what I'm going to do now, but I know it isn't going to be how it once was. You have an ideal, chase it down and finally grasp it in your hands only to see it disappear, and what do the rest expect you to do? They expect you to watch as it moves farther and farther away from you until it's gone entirely. I don't know if I'm capable.

The man shakes my hand, gives a weak smile. I nod and push the door open behind me, ushering him inside with my free hand. We're silent together, he and I, and I don't expect that to alter too much while he is in my home. His eyes look over our walls, his mouth slightly agape, nostrils flaring ever so slightly at the change of atmosphere, change of scent and scene alerting his senses. He crosses his arms over his chest while he walks on our wooden floors, echoes bouncing around the foyer, eyes never leaving our walls. I don't know what to do anymore, and this seems to be the only method worth exploring.

He'll give me five for the entire lot, a fair price. The words slither out of his mouth and spill onto our floors but there's no echo this time, only patient silence after he asks me what I think of his proposition. Five is excellent, five is more than I expected. Five is a fair price. I reach out my hand, shake his, and ask when he'll take it away? He stares at me, nods his head and says I can have an extra month if needed. Maybe he sees the pain behind my eyes, I'm not too sure. Maybe he knows he could've lowered the offer and gotten the same result, and he would've been right to do so, but maybe he knows a wounded animal is not worth aggravating.

I write, well wrote, for a living. Freelance when I was younger, legs fresh underneath me, world open and brand new. I fell in, hard the ground that was beneath my feet. Fell into a place I only anticipated and did not comprehend, not yet anyway. Nights spent hanging outside bars, clouds surrounding my head and my words mumbled, mouth lazy but eyes eager.

Sights unseen, drinks not drunk, pills not popped, not just yet. I was eighteen the night I first saw you, young and green and mind filled with the cloud that rested in front of my eyes so damn eager. I was eighteen, and you were twenty-three, and you did not know me and I did not you. Our eyes met for an instant, eagerness spent and the ground not so hard any longer. One day, I thought, maybe one day.

For five I wouldn't have to worry, but I don't think I want to live within these walls any longer anyhow. So many memories clumped together in one place, haunted dreams turned into haunted reality right before my eyes, dimmed and dirty from the rain. I would wipe away the water but I don't think I need to see our house again in this lifetime. Walking away is much easier, and with the five I can settle far north where the sun doesn't shine in the morning, where I won't need to greet it any more than I need to greet the world I used to know.

Circumstances create events I used to say in my talks, my speeches, my ramblings. You would turn around in your chair, laugh at me and say I was being far too serious again. I can't become a character in my own dream you'd tell me before turning back around and falling back into your world, into your work again. What separates me from a man on the page I wonder? Am I not as fake as he, forced to go about my life and pretend I care, pretend I am when I am far from not? Tired eyes are all I possess besides the five, and soon that will all be gone as well. Soon, but not now. I can cobble a life together, can believe in something somehow again. Not here, no, but somewhere.

Ours was a different type of love, this I still know. Take away my eyes from their sockets, take away my heart from my chest, take away my mind from my skull and this I will still know. A love built within our bones, built from the ground beneath our feet and sculpted from all around us, all that is. Take away all I know and I will still know our love for what it was and what it will be, wherever it may go now.

Keep you with me, my mind and body not strong enough to continue without it. The pain so real I feel with every step I take away from our house and into an unknown I never thought I would have to see alone. Tired eyes, no longer eager for the horizon, for what might wait and what might be. Tired eyes forced to move on, forced to find a new world in the ashes of the old.

Who would've guessed the brick wall of a bar would be my best friend for the years since we first saw each other that night? A depression entered my person and I couldn't shake it free. Replaced my thoughts with whiskey when I could get it, beer for when I could not. Replaced the booze with the drugs, replaced the drugs with more. Couldn't handle the hard ground I'd fallen on when I entered the world around me, and I kept falling without end.

A brick wall is a foundation of sorts, a haven against all others. Held me afloat when I fell and fell and fell, nights spent with my best friend at my back. I wanted to move out of the darkness and into the light. I wanted to shake what could not be un-shook from my bones, from my mind, from my soul. I needed you, and you weren't there. I needed you and I had only met you once, our eyes passing through a cloud of smoke.

Answers always seeming to be out of my reach, the dark only getting darker. Clawed my way into a clinic, pleading for a chance. Took the pills, took the medicine, took the dark and strangled it within my hands. Sessions, circles, coffee and sugar and just a hint of cream. Over and over the game I played, clawing further and further out of the dark that hypnotized my mind and paralyzed my person. Clawed my way from the hard ground I'd fallen on, clawed until I was able to walk again. I did not see the face of God, I did not see your face, I did not see any but my own. I was alone, cleaned of the dark and hand-in-hand with the light. I was alone, and I only knew who I was, not what I meant or where the path would lead me.

Work was difficult to come by, this I remember. Found a company, a place, a new haven, the wall no longer necessary. Bore into my work and it bore into me, staining my fingers, my hands with meaning again. Writing, how I missed the feeling of creation, of design, of a world built upon a promise worth keeping. Small, menial tasks at first, bosses over my shoulder and print left on the ground beneath my feet. Building toward something greater, something meaningful, something worthwhile. Rising further and further, the company growing, the world holding so much of the promise I thought I had created and kept in my head.

A decision had to be made, a decision of where I was going to be and of course, where I would find you. Your image had not left my mind. Though your eyes may have left mine after our brief meeting mine had not left yours, and I longed to know you, longed to see you again. Longed to reach out and gently dance my fingers along them before caressing your shoulders. Longed to know what your voice sounded like, longed to feel your heart beat across from mine and see life in all its splendor. Longed for a chance, an opportunity, and came to the conclusion, to the realization I was not the only one. A decision had to be made.

I left my new haven and worried I would be lost again into the dark. Shuttled forward and thrust down again onto the hard ground, falling a second time. The falling is easy, practical, but the need, the desire to get up from the ground again is much more difficult. Impossible if I had, but your image guided me. Nurtured me when I needed, helped me find my path, the true path. Helped me to see all I wanted, that all others would need, was a lifetime of promise. A promise, something you would not have to chase but that which could be yours entirely. People did not want the chase, no matter how much they pretended to. Fake, all fake, and I was the guide, the prophet, the holder of the key to unlocking the door of everlasting light. All I had to do was open the door, step inside, and I knew you would be waiting for me. This I knew.

How does one go about building an identity? They shape it from nothing and then shove it under the noses of those more powerful and more wealthy, exclaiming how great it can be. An identity in this world is more than just a business but an ideal, a chance, an opportunity. A reason to get out of the bed each morning and venture forth with the rest of mankind as if we all actually matter. My identity had to be crafted from the heavens, had to be visualized and put forth as making the unattainable attainable. All I needed was you, and I knew the only way to get you was through building this identity.

Using the funds from my previous employment I purchased a property in the city, an old warehouse on top of even less valuable land. Lunatic crossed my mind multiple times, the word clinging in my brain like the darkness I had left behind me. I didn't mind the word, thought it was fitting. A lunatic is what they would call me.

The next venture required my skills as a writer as well as establishing a connection. I had purpose this time when I ventured into the bars late at night and talked with power in sticky booths in unlit corners. Drinks bought, plans laid out on the table before them. Bold they called me, crazy to think it could actually work. I struggled to gain audience, struggled to gain an ear. I longed for the dark more than once, thought of it as a cool embrace rather than an icy plunge. Longed for the chance, the opportunity, until one evening it came in the form of a rather burly man wearing a slightly wrinkled suit with a desire for a relationship and a taste for top-shelf bourbon.

Government funding, how my luck had grown. Servers littered throughout the warehouse, programmers and engineers and all sorts of men and women roaming the once bare walls of my hastily purchased kingdom. A way to bring people together he had sputtered out in between heavy sobs, sobs of longing and compassion for a love he had once known. A way to bridge the gap, to build a connection. I smiled at what I had received, what I had concocted, what I had created. All it took was your face, and you did not know of course. You had no idea your eyes looking into mine would spawn a world turned on its head.

As a writer creating is essential, the backbone of any story, any printing, any paragraph of words I would throw down onto the page. A writer can hid behind their creation, use it to shape other characters or in this case other people. An idea is nothing more than a thought until action is taken, and then? Then it has the potential to become something extraordinary. I had moved so far in so little of time, and all because of one idea, one thought taken away from eyes seen through smoke. I was twenty-five, you were thirty, and our paths would only cross again because of an idea thought by eighteen year old me those many years ago: I wonder if she could possibly be my soulmate?

The rain falls steadily around me now, and you aren't here anymore. What does a creator have if the means for his greatest creation, the fuel behind th drive, is lost? Sealed in a casket six feet beneath the earth, the world swallowing you whole, reclaiming the flesh and blood and body I feel I had too little time with.

The five will last beyond me I believe, only because I know I will not look into the mirror and see anything worth spending it on. I know the dark will overcome me once more, the depression already settling back into roots it had known for a mere moment it seems, considering how much time has passed. I no longer wish to create, wish to write, wish to carry on what I've borne unto this world. I've tired eyes where once flashed eagerness, flashed meaning and hope and joy. I do not want to wipe the water from my eyes because when I am able to see clearly I will realize you are truly gone and never coming back. For this I confess I am weak. My bones feel heavy, my mind lost. I am hopeless, and without cause, and when I drive away from our house for the last time I will look out of stained glasses and try to piece together where the path will lead me next, my dream now a reality for the world, mine not one of them.

ABOUT THE AUTHOR

Shawn Miller is originally from Los Angeles. He currently lives in Colorado Springs.